The Bishop of Grunewald

A Tale from the Dungeon

FIRST EDITION

Jardonn Smith

The Bishop of Grunewald

A Tale from the Dungeon

FIRST EDITION

Published by The Nazca Plains Corporation
Las Vegas, Nevada
2006

ISBN: 978-1-887895-70-5

Published by

The Nazca Plains Corporation ®
4640 Paradise Rd, Suite 141
Las Vegas NV 89109-8000

PUBLISHER'S NOTE
The Bishop of Grunewald is a work of fiction created wholly by
the Jardonn Smith's imagination. All characters are fictional and
any resemblance to any persons living or deceased is purely
by accident. No portion of this book reflects any real person or
events.

Cover Art by PIGE
Art Direction, Blake Stephens

DEDICATION

Dedicated to all who are persecuted in their attempt to better human civilization.

The Bishop of Grunewald

A Tale from the Dungeon

Jardonn Smith

CONTENTS

THE BISHOP OF GRUNEWALD

THE BISHOP OF GRUNEWALD
Part One - The Bitter Tongue

There was a time when the church was all-powerful. Right or wrong, it was the only unifying force for the peasants of the western world, and it ruled with a dominating authority to keep them ignorant, fearful and obedient.

Such power in the hands of so few leads to abuse, and the little village of Grunewald was no exception, where the local Bishop was notorious for putting men to torture for the most trifling of reasons. Notice I said men and not women, because Bishop Frederick Bethune had no interest in wayward flock of the female persuasion. Women accused of heresy, witchcraft or any other abomination before the eyes of God might be simply strung up to dangle and rot, or better yet, burned at the stake, the idea being that only repentance would save them from certain death, which it never did or could.

But for men, Bishop Bethune preferred that they be given another chance, under torture, to renounce whatever evil thoughts had caused them to commit their misdeed. He sympathized with them, as he listened to the sounds of their screams and whimpers; he marveled at the sight of their naked bodies writhing and contorting in unholy agony; but mostly, he basked in the power of his authority. Breaking men down to beg for his mercy and forgiveness thrilled Frederick Bethune, for only with their anguished pleas would he restore their souls. Then, he would force them to swear silence as to how they were saved and allow them to return to the village, where they could live out the remaining years of their miserable lives.

This was his reputation, and whether the truth of his severity was accurate or exaggerated is irrelevant. The villagers of Grunewald lived with this fear and they were obedient. Only ones born of innately evil spirit dared to tempt his wrath. Those few who did painfully learned the truth for themselves.

This is the tale of three men: Jonathan Sikes; his life-long friend, William Corder; and William Corder's younger brother, Tobias. Oh, yes, mention should also be made of Helena, the wife of Jonathan Sikes, whose lust for what she should not have, as well as the evil-tongued lies she told in order to get what she should not have, led to the downfall of these three men.

The marriage of Jonathan Sikes to the woman Helena Morris was one of entrapment, instigated by her father Gregory to associate himself with Jonathan's father Sebastian. It was a question of wealth, if any holdings of a peasant could be considered wealth, but the income derived from the fields of wheat belonging to Sebastian Sikes far outweighed that of the six milk cows belonging to Gregory Morris.

At the behest of her father, Helena wooed the muscular and handsome young Jonathan into an impromptu tryst in the Morris barn, which in six weeks led to a claim of pregnancy and a demand of marriage. Fearing the wrath of Bishop Frederick Bethune, Sebastian Sikes convinced his son that he had best meet her demands and the sad ceremony took place in the Cathedral of Grunewald. Of course, poor Helena soon lost the child, evidence represented by the tissues of a bloody cyst removed from a Gregory Morris cow by Gregory Morris himself.

Helena never accepted her husband as being anything more than the man with whom she was forced to live, although any woman with any sense should have been attracted to his physical stature if nothing else. Jonathan Sikes was built like a manly beast of burden, thick and sturdy with massive chest, arms and legs. This physique came naturally to him at birth from generations of patriarchs named Sikes, whose backs were made broad by their work. The hard labor Jonathan performed every day to support his household only made him stronger.

Grunewald was surrounded by fields of wheat that once had been forest. Clearing trees, plowing earth and swinging sickle had built a prime specimen of masculine strength named Jonathan Sikes, but none of it impressed this woman. Regardless that he was her provider. Regardless that he performed his manly duties in their bed whenever called upon to do so, Helena quickly became restless. Nothing her husband could do would satisfy her yearnings. She was trapped in a loveless nightmare with a man not of her choosing, and inevitably her eyes and loins began to search for fulfillment elsewhere.

Her first attempt at extra-marital conquest was directed to William Corder, the constant companion of her husband. Friends since childhood, they both worked the fields, but William drove and cared for the wagons and teams of draft horses that were used either for planting or harvesting of crops. Slender and chiseled, his wiry physique was often present in the Sikes's household, where he and Jonathan would enjoy conversations over ale after a hard day's work. William had never married, preferring instead to satisfy the lonely and unattached women of the village. He did so with such skills that none of these women ever said a word to anyone, lest they spoil their good fortunes – and his.

All Helena needed was a few moments alone with him, and eventually the evening did come when William arrived at their home to meet Jonathan as usual, but his friend had yet to return from the fields. The frustrated Helena made her advance towards William, but was rebuffed.

"I'm sorry, Helena, your husband is my trusted friend. Do not ask me to betray him."

"Then, what of your brother, Tobias?" she coyly asked, as though William's rejection meant nothing to her. "Is he still a boy, or has he learned the ways of pleasing a woman?"

"My brother?" William sprang to his feet with a violence to send the chair tumbling. "Do not mention his name to me in this way. He is honest, pure of heart. I will not have him desecrated by the likes of you."

And so, the challenge was issued. Helena hatched a plot to seduce the man she truly wanted, young Tobias Corder. She had scrutinized him for the past several years, the fiery passion inside her intensifying with each passing day, as his body transformed from that of a boy to one of a strong, virile young man. As for Tobias, he had remained oblivious to the temptations of any and all females, focusing instead upon his apprenticeship with the village blacksmith, granted to him on the anniversary of his seventeenth year of life. Here he learned the art of shaping metal and swinging heavy hammers that broadened his back and bulked his torso.

This, however, was not what attracted Helena to young Tobias. Rather, it was his well-defined and bulging phallus. This is what caused her loins to ache. Majestically filling the crotch of his trousers in its flaccid state, the penis of this man, she fantasized, could only be an all-consuming tool when aroused, and Helena spent countless hours dreaming of what its dominating power could do to her. She was determined to have it, regardless of the protective threat issued by William Corder. Since she had failed in her initial scheme of gaining access to Tobias by first going through his older brother, she decided to eliminate the brother altogether.

High on a hill overlooking the village sat Egbert Castle, home of Peter Sion, lord and master to all peasants on his manse. His father had amassed the army to conquer this land, built his namesake castle above and Pope's cathedral below. From Egbert Castle, the elder Sion defended his belongings from all invaders who might lust for what was his – the village, the rich earth surrounding it and the virtual slaves who worked it. From here also came the evil reputation of Egbert Sion and the Rome-appointed Bishop.

The peasants saw the cathedral as holy and castle as evil, but a necessary evil. For the security provided by Egbert Sion and his soldiers, the villagers pretended not to notice when one of their fellow residents was dragged from their bed in the middle of the night, not to be seen again for days or weeks, always returned humbled and silent. They were dependent upon Sion for their survival; they were loyal to their Bishop as the appointed guardian of their faith; and they clung to their faith as the price of admission into the kingdom of heaven. Because of this, they trusted and obeyed the judgments and punishments of their Bishop without protest. No matter the violations, no matter the source of the accusations, a Bishop's word was blindly accepted as righteous, with or without proof, regardless of its severity.

With his father long since passed, Peter Sion ruled as the rightful successor, and in the castle, under the protection of Peter Sion, also lived his own Bishop of Grunewald, Frederick Bethune.

One day per week did the Bishop arrive by armed escort to the cathedral. This was the day all villagers attended mass, as Frederick Bethune performed the ceremonies himself, usurping these duties from the lowly priest. This was also a day to hear confessions, and since their Bishop was considered to be much closer to God than any priest, many villagers saved their confessions for this day, despite their belief that saying the wrong words could send them to the dungeons or worse.

It was here that Helena Sikes told her tale of woe. She sobbed while telling of how the demon-possessed William Corder had violated her sacred body, all at the behest, approval and witness of her very own husband. She screamed with fright when they dragged Jonathan Sikes from his bed, just before the next daybreak. Her skills of deception were flawless, as she pleaded with the soldiers not to take her husband from her, tearfully moaning that she could not survive without him, and she continued her charade until the armed men and their prisoner disappeared. She listened to the hooves of horses galloping up the hill to Egbert Castle, slowly closed the door and burst into laughter. Young Tobias Corder was hers for the taking.

Tank Books

Part Two – The Inquisition

When Jonathan Sikes was brought before Bishop Bethune, his friend William Corder was already there waiting. Jonathan had slept in loin cloth, while William slept in nothing, and this is how they now stood with their wrists roped behind their backs. The chamber was small and dark. Only one torch lit the room and it was positioned on the wall between two ornately carved stone benches, one occupied by Bishop Bethune and the other by Peter Sion, who always participated in these unpleasantries. Both benches rested on a raised platform, which allowed the two men to glare down at their prisoners with an air of dominating authority. Bethune wore an impressive, cream-colored robe with bold and wide, purple and gold borders circling collar and sleeves. Sion wore a robe of royal blue, with similar borders of solid black. The Bishop of Grunewald stood to read the accusations.

"William Corder, you are charged with desecration of the woman named Helena Sikes, forcing your evil phallus upon her, in her very own bed, against her will. How do you plead to these accusations?"

He looked to his friend in disbelief, shaking his head in sorrow. "Jonathan, you know I did not..."

"Do not address him," Bethune interrupted. "You will answer only to me and to God."

"I did not do this. She is the wife of my best..."

"I know who she is," again he barked. "She is a woman of faith. She is true to Jesus Christ and the Heavenly Father. She remains so, despite the defilement you have perpetrated upon her."

"I never touched her. These are lies."

"Enough! You must suffer for your sins. You must beg Our Father for forgiveness. Will you confess?"

"I've done nothing."

"Very well," the Bishop cast an evil grin, excited to see this man squirm.

Next, he turned to his other victim. "Jonathan Sikes, you are charged with violating your holy vows of matrimony, and with instigating the unwarranted assault upon your wife. What say you?"

He looked to William. "I know you did nothing. Helena has caused this. She has always hated..."

"Stop talking to him." Bishop Bethune stormed down the steps to stand before his prisoners, where he delivered a backhanded slap to the face of each. "Your fate rests with me, not with each other. Will you confess?"

Neither man moved to defend himself. They knew lashing out at a Bishop would be a fatal mistake, giving him legitimate authority to punish them.

"We have done nothing. He never touched her. She has lied. God knows this and so do you."

"Do not tell me what I know." Bethune ascended the steps to resume his position of superiority. "How dare you to assume what God knows and what God thinks. I will give you both one final opportunity. Will you confess your sins and beg for God's forgiveness?"

No answers were given, as both men cast their eyes to the cold, stone floor, knowing their fate was sealed.

"Then it is decided. William Corder and Jonathan Sikes, I hereby order that you both be put to torture, until which time you have confessed your sins and repented these evil deeds."

Bishop Bethune sat on his bench, bellowing an order to the guards standing near the only door in to or out of the chamber. "Bring my interrogators."

Three men – two of them brothers, one their cousin – were already waiting in the corridor and soon entered to take charge of their victims.

"Herman, that one is yours," Bethune pointed to Jonathan. "Otto and Oscar, he is yours. You know what to do, but first clean them up. They both smell like the beasts of burden they are."

And so, Herman led Jonathan Sikes from the chamber, accompanied by one of the standing guards. His cousins, the brothers Otto and Oscar, took hold of William, but before they could exit Peter Sion spoke. "William Corder, I hear rumors that you have bedded many women in your time. Is this true?"

He hesitated, deciding it best to tell the truth. "When asked."

"Helena Sikes did not ask, yet you had your way with her."

"No, sire, I did not. She has told these lies out of vengeance."

"Vengeance for what?"

"She wants my brother. I vowed she would never have him."

"Ah, your brother is Tobias?"

"Yes."

"The young blacksmith?"

"Yes."

Sion said nothing. He merely nodded to Bishop Bethune, who spoke to the henchmen. "Take him to the steps, after he was been washed of his filth."

William Corder was led down the same corridor, then stairwell that had been traversed by Jonathan Sikes and his escorts. Foolishly, William had hoped that the truth might save them, but the men who controlled their fate were not interested in the truth. They were only interested in exploiting the masculine power of the male physique, a commodity of which Jonathan and William, in their own unique forms, possessed in prime-grade abundance.

Part Three – The Little Bull

"So, the woman thinks she is clever," Bishop Bethune addressed his friend and keeper, Peter Sion. The two of them remained seated, now alone in the Chamber of Inquisition.

"Yes, Frederick. Why do these foolish men fall prey to such treachery?"

"They think with their penis," Bethune mocked. "They have no brain."

"It is our good fortune that it is so."

"True, Peter, these two are not like the petty thieves and weasels who have come before them. These men have backbone. I doubt either of them will be easily broken."

"Yes, the supposed exploits of William Corder have interested me for quite some time," Sion licked his lips. "And as for Jonathan Sikes, well, his powerful physique speaks for itself."

"Fate has brought them to you, Peter. Perhaps one of your potions might be useful. Did you see what dangles between William's legs? It is a penis perfectly shaped and sized for any activity, and apparently it is well-versed in the performance of its manly duties."

"So I have heard. I will enjoy putting his manhood to the test."

"I give them both to you," Bishop Bethune offered while rising from his bench. "Come, you'd best take charge of our interrogators.

Otherwise, nothing will be left of our handsome prisoners."

This was a good-natured joke between the men, if such a thing is possible when referring to torture, because Oscar, Herman and Otto were not allowed to begin the questioning until orders were given to do so by Bethune or Sion.

Exiting the chamber, the Bishop and his protector prepared to go separate ways. "Will you be joining us, Frederick?"

"In time. First, there are a few administrative duties that require my attention."

"Very well. Time is not an issue with these two." Sion turned to traverse the corridor taken by the prisoners, while Bethune climbed the stairs that would take him to his living quarters and office.

Peter Sion was approaching his sixth decade of life. He had assumed the throne three decades prior and sired an appropriate heir too. This was done by summoning females he found minimally attractive from the village to receive his seed until the desired male offspring was delivered to him. With that duty fulfilled, he turned his attention to assisting with interrogations of male prisoners, while keeping his son – and the two daughters that preceded him in birth – headquartered in the upper reaches of the castle, far removed from the shenanigans in his torture chamber.

He had no interest or respect for females not related to him, which was not uncommon for men of his stature. Peter had adopted this attitude from his father, who saw them as nothing more than vessels to produce necessary offspring. Only then did they deserve the tender affections of a man, and that was merely to instigate copulation. Other than that, they were here to serve men as slaves. In the castle, women performed the mundane duties that were beneath men, such as cleaning of floors, walls, fixtures, living spaces and clothing. Only male staff prepared the food and only men served it. Women were not trusted with such vital functions.

Education and raising of children was done by men. The kitchen was run by men. The dungeon cells and torture chamber were kept in top condition by men. For the past twenty-two years, the men in charge of Sion's dungeon had been Herman, Otto and Oscar. They were soldiers of Peter Sion's army, and he himself had carefully chosen them for this duty.

The three knew their boundaries as to what extremes of punishment a man's body could take, based on his age, musculature and health. They, like Sion and Bethune, relished the sights and sounds of men in bondage. To them, it was a challenge to see how much a man could withstand, to push him to the limits of endurance, to break his spirit, while keeping him attentive in hopes that he would continuously spout words of defiance and manly resolve. Herman and his cousins were not, however, allowed to inflict any sorts of crippling damage to organs or bones, nor permanent scars to the skin – not without the permission of Bethune or Sion. These foul deeds were reserved for the whims of the Bishop and his protector, when and if such atrocities became necessary.

Jonathan and William were taken to a dark room of stone, where Oscar, Otto and Herman locked them into leg irons attached to chains that were bolted to the floor. After stripping Jonathan of his loin cloth, they proceeded to scrub down both of their prisoners with warm water, soap and horse-hair brushes. Jonathan was outfitted with a metal bar four feet in length. This was placed to the back of his neck and held in place by Otto, while Herman and Oscar secured his wrists to the bar with straps of cowhide two inches in width. The straps were fringed on their edges with thin strips, which were tied together to tighten the straps around Jonathan's wrists, thus securing him to the metal bar.

They unlocked his leg iron and led him clean and dry from the holding cell to the torture chamber. Jonathan inspected the instruments of pain surrounding him, and with each one he saw he imagined what he would feel. He envisioned himself bound to one device after another and the punishments he would have to endure. Terror seized him. With a burst of fear-induced adrenaline he tried to bolt from his captors.

Jonathan gave a powerful kick to Otto, sending him to stagger forward. Then he tried to turn and run for the door, but a swift lifting of the metal bar took his feet from the floor. Herman and Oscar stood strong with arms stretched over their heads, rendering Jonathan's legs useless for running. All he could do was kick, which is exactly what he did.

He bent his knees and back-kicked their legs with his bare feet. He targeted their knees, which nearly caused them to collapse, until Otto quickly approached from behind to grasp first one and then the other of Jonathan's ankles. Otto clamped both shins between his powerful arms and rib cage, then stepped back, bringing Jonathan with him and stretching his prisoner's upper body into full suspension.

"Stop this, Sikes," Otto growled. "There is no escape. You know this."

"Damn you. I've done nothing." He abandoned his physical struggle and relaxed his legs. "Let me go."

"We cannot do that. It is not our concern. We are to prepare you for interrogation. Do not make things worse than they already are."

Otto was correct. It was useless and Jonathan did know this all along, but he had to try. Oscar, Herman and Otto had expected it, were prepared for it and respected their prisoner for attempting what they themselves would do if they were in his circumstance.

Upon entry to the torture chamber, a look to the left showed a large section of roughened wood, which was bolted to the stone wall. Standing vertical, this rectangular board measured ten feet tall by five feet wide. Near the top, two metal, L-shaped hooks protruded from its wood surface. Their extension length from the wood was three inches, while vertical length upwards was six. These hooks were spaced three feet apart. Near the bottom, two sets of thick chains were bolted to the wood surface, each comprised of three chain links. Bolted to each chain were hinged leg irons, opened and waiting for ankles.

Otto let go of Jonathan's legs and the other two lowered the bar for him to stand upright, no longer struggling against them. Otto positioned two, five-step ladders against the wall on either side of the board and with metal bar in their grasps, Herman and Oscar climbed. As they ascended their ladders, they brought Jonathan's arms with them until their height lifted his body from the floor. Continuing their climb, Herman and Oscar reached the level of the two hooks and placed the bar to rest on their horizontal extensions inside the upward vertical extensions, leaving Jonathan to hang from the bar. Below him at floor level, Oscar encompassed both of his ankles into the leg irons and clamped them shut. The bondage of Jonathan Sikes was complete.

He was vertically suspended, his arms and legs flared wide to form the letter X. His feet dangled in irons eighteen inches from the floor, and although his legs were not stretched tight, the chain links prevented him from drawing them upwards beyond two inches. His chest protruded towards the center of the room, while his back lightly touched the rough wood behind him. Gravity stretched him and this caused his middle section to flatten, while the small of his back curved out from the wood.

The three henchmen were nearly finished with their task, but not quite.

It was by order of Peter Sion that all victims of torture be outfitted with the official color of Egbert Castle, royal blue. This was done by way of a loin covering, which served to subjugate the victims and remind them to whom they belonged. Plus, the coverings were designed in a way to isolate and control a man's penis. The fitting was tight, so that the outlines of the man's cock head could easily be seen, yet the actual details tantalizingly concealed. It also served as a guide for the three interrogators, as the cloth followed the lines of a man's pelvic bone, leaving the meat of his belly fully exposed. Above the line was fair game. Below and beneath the cloth was forbidden. Finally, one more very important need existed for the loin covering, and that was as a precautionary measure. Odds were good that a tortured man would involuntarily evacuate either urine or feces during the process and the cloth was there to collect the man's waste, which was far preferable to having it soil the equipment or the interrogators or both. With cloth removed, victim washed and a fresh cloth to replace the ruined, a man's torture could continue just as it had begun.

Jonathan's groin was reachable from the floor, and while Otto outfitted him with his loin cloth, Herman and Oscar removed the ladders and stacked them in the corner to Jonathan's right. This is how they left him. The three exited and returned to the room where William was waiting in leg iron, still dripping with water and wondering where they had taken his friend – and what was planned for him.

Peter Sion had chosen these three to run his dungeon and torture chamber for sound reasons. First, they were men not far removed in appearance from their ancient, cave-dwelling ancestors. Protruding foreheads, over-sized jowls and ears, massive chests, arms and legs, plus gorilla-like fur defined their bodies. They were short and compact, ranging in height from Otto's five feet and seven inches to Oscar's five feet and nine. Their powerful forms were mesmerizing and intimidating when seen by men that were to be tortured. And as a way to further fill his victims with dread, Sion insisted that Otto, Oscar and Herman perform their interrogations with every inch of their brutish bodies in full view.

Not only were men under torture presented with three apish physiques, but also three menacing penises, each generously endowed with such length and width that they swung side to side when the men walked – sometimes streaming urine, sometimes flinging pre-cum. Adding to this, the stifling heat and poor circulation of air in the torture chamber instantly caused their skin to glisten with sweat, while their hairy coats became matted and sparkling with streams of briny drippings.

All combined, the image of these three mountains of masculinity

– these three alpha-males – caused a chained man to fear them more than the torture to come.

Another reason Peter Sion chose these men was for the close bonds that the three felt amongst one another – not just by blood, but by mutual admiration. This was further perpetrated by Sion, who did not allow his henchmen access to any females. Only after a successful interrogation would they be rewarded with female servants brought for their enjoyment, and even then they were given only 48 hours before the females would be taken away.

So, until another session of torture was completed, Oscar, Herman and Otto lived their lives alone and were forced to discover new ways to please themselves. They learned to admire one another. They enjoyed seeing each other sweat when they worked, as muscles were strained to manipulate whatever implements of torture they used. With visions of their punishment performances always fresh in their minds, Oscar, Otto and Herman satisfied one another's desires with nightly get-togethers in their shared sleep chamber near the room of torture.

It took two to satisfy one and in the beginning it was strictly manual. One would lay on his back to receive hand rubs to his chest and belly, coupled with finger rubs to his nuts and hand strokes to his penis. Once orgasm was achieved, another would take his place, sprawling on his back to receive the same treatment. Of course, this manual stimulation could not alone satisfy for long and oral worship came into play, with kissing, licking and sucking discovered to be even more gratifying, especially when combined with the rubbing of rough, masculine hands.

And in time, thanks to the isolation forced upon them by Peter Sion, these three discovered that the anus was a fair substitute for a vagina. None of them had any qualms of either accepting or performing such an act. Otto, Oscar and Herman became inseparable, loyal to one another with no jealousies between them. And because their lives were far more pleasant and preferable to the existence of a mere foot soldier, whose time was mostly spent standing guard for endlessly dull hours indoors and outdoors in weather good or bad, these three men extended their loyalty to Peter Sion with the same fervor they applied to one other.

Of all good reasons to have these men in his torture chamber, intelligence was the vital element of importance to Peter Sion. Despite their brutish appearance, Oscar, Herman, and especially Otto were very clever men. They had proven it on the battlefield many times, and in one instance, the three had alone practically saved the realm of Peter Sion with their strength and cunning.

It took place on Runyan Bridge and it was Otto's idea. On one side of the River Runyan was open valley and the realm of Count Bernard; on the other, rock cliffs, the realm of Peter Sion. These cliffs and the river framed the road in question. After crossing the bridge, this road immediately turned to the right, as the cliffs towered to the left and ahead of it. The road continued along the cliffs for a few hundred yards, and then curved to the left to make its way through Runyan Pass. This was a divide of fifty feet in width, flanked by rock cliffs of thirty feet in height on either side. Beyond this, nothing but forests and open fields, as the road traversed another forty miles to the village of Grunewald and Egbert Castle.

With the river far too deep and wide to cross with battlements and armored soldiers, Count Bernard's success of invasion rested upon crossing of the bridge, an endeavor of which he had tried and failed six times. Each battle had been meaningless stalemates, with Bernard's soldiers occasionally making their way onto Sion's side of the bridge, only to be counterattacked and pushed back. Peter Sion had no interest in Bernard's holdings, nor did he have interest in the tiresome defending of the bridge. He was bored. He wanted to go home, so when his attache announced that one of his soldiers had a plan of action, Sion was willing to listen.

"His name is Otto, but they call him the little bull."

"Why?" Sion scoffed. "Is he lacking in the groin?"

"No, sire. It is his stature."

"Very well. I will listen." Peter Sion had little interest in soldiering or in soldiers, until this man entered his tent. Short, indeed, but to Peter, Otto was peculiarly masculine. A perfectly round head was topped by short black hair, over-sized ears were flared as though butterfly wings, and bulging biceps and forearms suspended hands shaped like boulders. Sion imagined that whatever was hidden beneath his breastplate must be as beautifully shaped as the breastplate itself.

"So, Otto, little bull... tell me of your plan."

Peter Sion thought the idea was foolhardy, but also figured if it didn't work the only harm done would be the death of a few more soldiers on both sides. Since he was disinterested and had no better strategies of his own, Peter agreed to Otto's plan.

Luring Bernard's men into charging the bridge was no problem, because this time they were met with only token resistance. They made impressive progress, pushing Sion's soldiers back from the bridge, around the curve of the road, along the cliffs and into the pass. Here, a legion of Sion's army attacked from above with nets and with arrows, but Bernard's men held firm in a defensive posture with shields overhead. They cut away the nets and maintained position against Sion's men, who descended the cliffs and attacked from behind in an attempt to seal the invaders to the pass.

Unbeknownst to Bernard's soldiers doing battle in Runyan Pass, Otto, Oscar and Herman had hidden themselves beneath Runyan Bridge. Otto, stripped naked but for his loin cloth, was climbing and crawling from one wooden support to another, hacking at their joints with his heavy sword, while Herman and Oscar waited between connecting trusses and the underside of the roadbed at Sion's end of the bridge.

In the valley, Count Bernard sat on his horse flanked by his escort of twelve. He, not being the bravest of souls, never joined in the battle, instead staying safely behind until his army had cleared the way.

One of his entourage spotted the whiteness of Otto's loin cloth.

"Sire, look," a soldier pointed. "There is a man beneath the bridge."

"What is he doing?" Bernard was puzzled.

"It appears... he's hacking at the wood."

"They aim to destroy it. He must be stopped."

Bernard's twelve men reared their horses and streaked for the bridge, just as Herman, Oscar and Otto knew they would. Herman and Oscar climbed from their underneath hiding place in full battle dress. With swords, bows and arrows hidden in nearby brush, they streaked for their weapons and waited for Bernard's men to come within range. Two on foot battled twelve on horseback near the Barnard end of Runyan Bridge, while Otto continued to weaken the supports beneath.

Meanwhile, with Bernard's army gradually pushed forward by the one legion Sion had devoted to that project, the full force of Peter Sion's army charged out of the forest. They rushed towards the opposite side of the pass and head-on into the army of Count Bernard, pushing them back with great speed. Hopelessly trapped and with their numbers dwindling, a retreat was ordered and Bernard's men fought their way through Sion's one legion, working themselves out of the pass the way they had entered. Around the curve they went, retracing the ground earlier taken, while the full army of Peter Sion pursued their behinds.

As Runyan Bridge came into their view, Oscar and Herman stood firm, having incapacitated seven of Bernard's twelve soldiers. Then came an ear-piercing whistle, the signal, followed by a shout from below.

"It is time. Retreat!"

With a horrific groan, the supports gave way and the bridge buckled.

Herman and Oscar scrambled for the nearest end to them, which was the Bernard side, as the bridge's roadbed cracked and tilted, but did not fall.

Bernard's army was approaching from the pass not more than one minute away and Otto had to work quickly. He climbed to the main, Sion-side truss and hacked again with his sword. He pressed his hands underneath the flat roadbed surface, angled his bare feet perpendicular to the rounded, thirty-degree-angled, wooden truss, and pushed with all his might. Otto's powerful arms pushed upwards, while his massive legs pressed downwards. His mighty chest and belly sent exertion to both and the main truss gave way, taking all connections with it like collapsing dominoes. The roadbed and all that supported it tumbled into the River Runyan, leaving Bernard's army no escape.

Some of them jumped into the river, where their heavy armor took them directly to the bottom. Most were slaughtered on the road with no bridge, as Sion's army moved forward to hack and skewer one after another of Bernard's men.

Herman and Oscar were trapped on Bernard's side of the bridge. Three of the seven still living when the bridge collapsed went with it, which left only four of Bernard's soldiers for Oscar and Herman to defeat – a challenge easily met. Only Bernard remained. He sat motionless on his horse, watching the obliteration of his army on the other side of the river until Herman and Oscar requested his sword. The Count offered no resistance.

From Sion's realm, Peter squinted to see Bernard standing defenseless, flanked by Herman and Oscar with swords raised to the heavens. Peter Sion raked his thumb across his throat. Herman raked his sword across the throat of Count Bernard.

There were no prisoners taken on this day. Sion and his army made ready to return home, leaving all dead to lie where they fell. Herman and Oscar stripped to their loin cloths and swam the River Runyan, where dangling ropes greeted and lifted them onto Sion soil.

Of course, all were saddened by the loss of Otto, but the little bull died a hero. He was eulogized by Frederick Bethune in the Grunewald Cathedral. He was memorialized by Peter Sion in Egbert Castle. Five days after his glorious victory at Runyan Bridge, with his army dressed in full regalia, assembled in an open courtyard inside the main castle gates, Peter Sion was interrupted in his tribute to Otto by a shouting outside of those gates.

"Open the door. I have one of your men."

A horse-drawn wagon entered which contained the sleeping, naked form of the little bull. He had taken a ride on that truss all the way down to the river, somehow avoiding the falling debris around him. That same truss had been his ride downstream for two miles, until he spotted a tree near the riverbank with roots exposed. Leaving his transport, he swam to and climbed those roots, then his bare feet took him the next eighteen miles. There, he found a farmhouse with a farmer and food and drink and wagon, which took him the final twenty miles to Egbert Castle.

Otto's survival did not diminish his hero status. In fact, the respect he enjoyed was elevated when it was learned that he had spent time with remnants of Bernard's supporters. The tree he had climbed to exit the river was on the wrong side of that river, and although he avoided all humans the first day, on the second he was captured. Otto was tortured, but never broken, and with cunning and trickery, he finagled his escape. It is a story only Otto can tell, when the little bull has a mind to do so.

Who better to assist Peter Sion with his interrogations than Otto and his brother and his cousin? They would forever be soldiers whenever any serious soldiering was required, but more than this, they were Sion's most trusted men. The four of them worked together as a fine-tuned team, both in the field and in the torture chamber.

The Battle of Runyan Bridge was the last serious threat to Peter Sion's realm for the remainder of his years. After all, who would dare challenge his power with such men at his disposal?

Part Four - The Steps to Purgatory

Alone and hanging, Jonathan scanned the torture room. It was constructed of different sized and shaped heavy stones mortared together, with distance from floor to ceiling approximately 20 feet. The room was near-square and 30 feet separated parallel walls. Directly across from him was a wooden stairwell that, oddly enough, ascended to the solid wall where no opening existed. An openhearth fireplace with fire burning was cut into the wall to its left, and further left, near the wall perpendicular to Jonathan's, was a round wooden table. With its surface horizontal, the height was four feet and circumference twelve. Four ropes came from four directions, each extending from four wooden mounts near the table's edge. Each mount held at its side one saw-toothed metal gear, with wooden handle attached to the gear.

Throughout the room, pairs of chains with wrist irons attached dangled from the ceiling, while pairs of chains with leg irons attached laid on the floor. Also on the floor near the walls were leather whips, wooden clubs and wooden, spear-like poles, plus other unpleasant items that could be used for beating the sense in to or out of hapless victims.

Fortunately or not, the solitude granted Jonathan Sikes lasted for but a few minutes. Peter Sion entered to absorb the sight of his powerful prisoner. He was dressed as though going on a hunt, but with jacket removed. A tan-colored, linen shirt was tucked into belted, brown wool trousers, which were tucked into black, mid-calf height boots. Silently, he strolled from one side of the board to the other, marveling at the glorious, masculine specimen bound and suspended before him. Scanning every inch of stretched muscle, he searched for what might be the pinnacle of the man's strength. Unlike most interrogators, who attacked the weakest point, Peter Sion preferred to break down the most formidable defense he could find, and Jonathan unwittingly helped his tormentor in this regard.

This strong man flexed his body in a useless attempt to break free. His chest expanded, his muscular arms and legs strained, which caused the well-defined ripples and curves of his meaty middle section to explode. These muscles revealed themselves.

The eyes of Peter Sion were immediately drawn to his prisoner's belly. He focused on the thick, sculptured muscle between rib cage and pelvic bone. He placed the tips of his fingers onto the skin surface and began to knead those muscles as though they were a loaf of bread.

"Mmm, solid as the walls of this room, Jonathan Sikes. I do believe yours is the finest belly ever given to a man, but it won't be when I am finished with it. Do you wish to speak, or shall we begin?"

Jonathan recoiled from the man's touch, sucking in his abdomen and tightening it with all his strength, "I have done nothing. Get your hands off of me."

Sion brought his second set of fingers to join the first, digging them deeper into the powerful muscle. "That board against your back has a name. I call it my Board of Impalement. Do you know why?"

"I don't care. You know I am innocent. Why do you keep me here?"
"Save your denials for your Bishop. They are of no concern to me."

"Then what do you want of me?"

"I want your strength. I want to see you perform."

"You'll get nothing."

"We shall see about that." Sion removed all fingers and stepped back to further admire the god-like sculpturing of belly muscle. "Remain defiant as long as you wish, Jonathan Sikes. I will enjoy seeing your belly ground to a pulp."

With lower jaw thrust forward and an impressive flexing of all muscles, Jonathan accepted his tormentor's challenge. "Do your worst."

"My worst is exactly what you will get."

And with that, Peter Sion exited the room. He would plan his strategy against one victim while overseeing preparations made for the other.

When Frederick Bethune had ordered his henchmen to take William Corder to the steps, he was not referring to any stairwell, but rather, the device he and Peter Sion affectionately called the Steps to Purgatory.

Situated against the opposing wall to where Jonathan Sikes was hanging on his board, the Steps to Purgatory was a descending set of rough, wooden planks built as though stairs to nowhere, unless one could walk through solid stone. With the upper end bolted to one wall, the series of boards and two perpendicular runners to which they were connected angled down, until the opposing ends reached the floor. The steps were spaced about one foot apart from each other in height and their length between the runners was five feet. Some of their edges were sharp and precise, while others had been roughened and splintered.

In reality, the Steps to Purgatory was a stretch rack. William was placed upon the steps and made to lay on his back by Otto and Oscar, while Herman and Peter Sion stood nearby. Approximately twenty-five feet directly across from him, Jonathan hung strapped to his board helplessly watching them fix his friend to the center of this contraption.

William's body was parallel with the two runners, his back side flowing down the series of steps, sharp and rough edges pressing into his skin. His feet were positioned above, while the rest of him followed the angle of the device downwards, leaving his head to dangle between the fourth and fifth lowest of the step-like boards.

The fourth step from the top was missing, replaced by a wooden axle with holes drilled through. Ropes dangled from two of these holes, knotted at one end to anchor them to the axle. With plenty of space between the runners and prisoner on either side, Otto climbed the steps and tied the free ends of two ropes to William's ankles, leaving a hint of slack in each. Below, Herman did the same with the victim's wrists, securing two ropes by knotting them to the lowest step. He left no slack in these ropes, stretching William's arms in straight lines beyond and below his head and spaced one foot apart.

Peter Sion was more than impressed with the sight he had created. William's chiseled physique came to life in its downward sloping and tightened position. With arms extended past his head and parallel to each other, his deltoids expanded and the sinewed muscle in his chest, stomach and belly were clearly defined. His torso from belly to arm pits assumed the shape of an inverted and curved V, while his flaccid peter rested comfortably atop his healthy balls as though a nested egg of incubation waiting to hatch.

As Otto descended the steps, Oscar climbed with royal blue loin covering in hand, but was interrupted by Peter Sion.

"Wait." Sion climbed the steps opposite the side where Oscar stood, leaned down and lifted his victim's penis between finger and thumb. "It is too beautiful to cover."

William recoiled at the tormentor's touch, raising his head to protest. "What are you doing? Get your hands off of me."

"No," he sneered. "I cannot decide where it should rest." He let go the penis and allowed it to fall onto William's belly, gravity naturally forcing it to follow the downward angle of the steps. Sion descended to inspect the view, pacing the floor and absorbing the scene from every possible angle.

"Better for your cock to rest on the testicles. It will snake its way onto your belly soon enough." He climbed the steps to lay the peter onto William's balls, slightly pressing down so that the skin of his cock would stick to the skin of his nuts, holding the masterpiece in defiance of gravity.

Outside the runner to William's right was a spoked, wooden wheel, which was attached to the end of the wooden axle. The six spokes extended past the rim of the wheel by twelve inches and the wheel itself was parallel to the runner of the steps. Because the axle of the wheel was nearly six feet above the floor surface, Oscar was the designated controller of this wheel, he being the tallest of the three. Standing barefooted at five feet, nine inches in height, he reached up at the command of Peter Sion to grasp a spoke and turn the wheel. Once slack was taken from the rope, Oscar pushed upwards with all his strength and displayed himself. The massive muscles in his chest, triceps and deltoids flexed to capacity, as his tremendous power unleashed all energy upon the resistance of the wheel.

And what was causing this resistance? The stretched form of William. The ropes wrapped around his ankles pulled his body away from the stationary ropes wrapped around his wrists. His back side was dragged inches up the steps, his skin scraped and splintered. His front side was a strained, yet beautiful line of elongated muscle, as he valiantly struggled against the ropes in order to hold his body together. William's voice echoed throughout the torture chamber in conjunction with his exertion, growling and groaning in tones of masculine resistance.

Peter Sion and his men enjoyed these sights and sounds. William's struggle nearly caused them to drool and their excitement was intensified with the knowledge that this was a mere sample, just a test to see how the man would react and what his body would look like when stretched. The appearance of William under torture was beyond Sion's greatest expectations, but before he could order Oscar to release the wheel, a shout came from across the room.

"Stop, you bastards. You're going to rip him apart."

With a wave of Sion's hand, Oscar let go the wheel and the stretching of William was stopped. Slowly, painfully, his body inched back down the steps, his back side absorbing more wooden splinters along the way.

"So, Jonathan Sikes," Sion turned to walk towards him. "Feeling neglected, are you? Do you think I would destroy your companion so soon? I am much more clever than that."

He motioned for Herman to join him. They both stood before the suspended man, whose anguish over what he had just seen caused him to again uselessly struggle against his bondage.

"Look at this, Herman." Sion repeated the kneading of Jonathan's belly muscle with his fingers. "Feel the powerful wall beneath his skin."

Herman did the same with his clawed fingertips. "Hard as stone."

"Yes, indeed it is. I think impalement might be the order of the day. Use your spear."

Part Five - The Trickster

Helena wasted no time in seducing young Tobias Corder. As soon as daylight broke and she heard the distant clanking of metal on metal, she fancied herself up and strolled towards the blacksmith shop. Three times that morning she interrupted his work, teasing and wooing him until the blacksmith in charge shooed her away. Planting seeds she was, always hovering nearby and finagling herself to remain in his sights, so that when work was stopped for the noontime meal, Tobias came to her. The sleeping giant inside his trousers was awakened. He surrendered.

Helena led him by the hand with no shame or concern for who saw what or thought what, and Tobias followed with no concern for anything besides the satisfaction of his penis. He had no knowledge that this woman's husband and his own brother were at that very moment suffering in the dungeons of Egbert Castle. It would not have mattered even if he had known. Helena had effectively mesmerized the young man into a lust-filled trance, with no awareness of anyone or anything other than himself. Even the importance of his apprenticeship at the blacksmith shop was forgotten, as fantasies of his first-time foray into the female bosom danced in his head. It was just as Bishop Bethune and Peter Sion had said in regards to men in the village of Grunewald. Tobias Corder allowed his penis to do his thinking.

That afternoon he felt the warm, wet, tenderly squeezing confines of the female vagina, while Helena felt the incredible, all-consuming strength of his mighty cock. Initially, the young man's exploration was a bit awkward, but the pent-up yearning of his lady partner quickly soothed all apprehensions. With each dominating stroke, the confidence of Tobias grew and he began to feel. He felt her vaginal walls crushing him at his deepest penetration, clamping him in her vise and valiantly resisting his retraction. He felt her vibrating clitoris rubbing his massive corona, as he scraped against it from both directions in and out. And just as he felt his balls shrinking in preparation to jettison their bounty, the door was burst open and the naked Helena and Tobias were confronted by the soldiers of Peter Sion.

In an instant, Helena screamed and begged for them not to take her man, but this time the wretched woman meant what she said. Jolted from the heights of ecstasy to the horrors of betrayal in seconds, she collapsed to her knees, alternating moans with shrieks. She bloodied her hands in a maddened frenzy of woeful fists, pounding them against the stone surfaced floor. And once again she listened to the familiar echo of horse hooves fading outside her open door.

Clever, was she? Perhaps, but not half as clever as the good Bishop Bethune. He who holds the power is the most clever of all, and if Helena Sikes did not yet understand this, she soon would.

In the torture chamber, Helena's husband had his own problems, as Herman taunted the hapless Jonathan Sikes. With wooden pole in his hand, the hulking ape menacingly paced in front of his victim. His weapon resembled a spear, its length five feet, its thickness two inches. At one end the edge was flat, but at the other it tapered to a blunt, rounded point of one-half of an inch.

Despite this threat, Jonathan was not intimidated. He mentally prepared himself. He tensed his abdominal muscles in a posture of defense, expanding his chest and flattening his middle, but when Herman unleashed his assault it came with well-targeted effectiveness. He drove the blunt point into the lower depths of Jonathan's belly, midway between his navel and groin. With a two-fisted grip on the middle of his spear, Herman thrust the impaler forward with meaty forearms, biceps and triceps, while leaning into the opposite end of the spear with his chest.

Nearby stood Sion. He slowly paced on either side of Herman, taking in the view and the sounds from all angles. Both were mesmerizing. His prisoner's teeth were exposed and clinched, deep, guttural grunts of exertion seeping between them. He strained his arms to lift himself those two minuscule inches as a way to further tighten his belly. His chest expanded and pectorals bulged, while fists clinched and toes curled.

Jonathan Sikes was everything Sion had hoped. A physique impressively thick and sturdy in its natural state had elevated to the physique of a manly god, comprised of sculptured muscle symmetrically balanced with deep-ridged lines and curves. A navel with knot naturally hidden now revealed its former feeding tube, as the muscle beneath forced it forward, framed and centered by the elongated skin of its stretched belly button rim. Man-tits normally parked beneath curved pectorals and pointing downward now were lifted and stretched, perfectly round and reddish brown.

Sion did manage to conceal his lust in order to verbally taunt. "There is your answer, Jonathan Sikes. The Board of Impalement. How does it feel?"

There could be no answer. All energy, all thought was concentrated to his belly, as Jonathan's abdominal wall held back the penetrating pole.

"Herman, I believe he has had an adequate taste." The pole was withdrawn and Herman caught his breath – as did Jonathan Sikes, but not for long.

"You may now pepper him, Herman." Sion spoke in a casual tone as though requesting his dinner. "I'd say twelve should do."

With an altering of his grip to an under-handed left in front, and an over-handed right behind, Herman thrust his pole forward in a jabbing spear attack. He pierced the muscle with pinpoint accuracy, then quickly released and speared again. His skills were impressive, as he penetrated the belly muscle from just above the pelvic bone to the navel, both sides and the entire length, never once striking anything but Jonathan's tightened wall of resistant meat.

Deep thuds of wood penetrating muscle accompanied deep grunts of guttural resistance, as Jonathan absorbed and resisted the mighty thrust of Herman's spear. Twelve impalements were ordered and twelve were given, but on the tenth, William cried out for his friend just the same as Jonathan had done for him.

And what did William receive for his concern? Another stretching. As Jonathan recovered from the cruel spearing of his belly, William howled and struggled to keep his tendons and joints from pulling apart. Soon, protests were heard between gasps of air coming from across the room. Jonathan again pleaded for them to stop torturing poor William, at which time Herman drove home his spear to resume his torture of Jonathan.

The pattern was established. Pleading for mercy on behalf of his companion only brought more punishment for the man who did the pleading. It was a test of their friendship, a design of trickery concocted by Peter Sion. This was no interrogation, because no questions were asked. Sion wanted to know the depths of their loyalty to one another. Which man would abandon the other? Which man would be the first to remain silent? Which man would allow the other to be tortured, so that he would be spared?

Peter Sion stood centered between both men and never said a word. Herman and Oscar knew what to do and how to do it, which allowed Sion to relish the sights and sounds all around him. Not only could he enjoy the two men who suffered, but by this time his henchmen also were drenched in sweat. Oscar and Herman only intensified the drama. In fact, Sion was nearly ecstatic with what he had created. Two tortured men, one naked, one with loin covering, displayed their glorious physiques in heroic resistance. Two tormentors, both naked, flared their powerful, glistening muscles to inflict more punishment. The torture chamber oozed masculinity. The smells, sounds and sights of men hard at work and hard at suffering nearly brought frothing to the mouth of Peter Sion.

He watched and he waited and he fought himself, struggling to suppress his urge to strip away his own clothing and reveal to them his true excitement. These two men, Jonathan Sikes and William Corder, performed for him like none before them. They never abandoned one another – never silenced their protests in defense of one another, and in so doing they pushed Herman and Oscar to their limits of endurance. The bonds of Jonathan and William were not to be broken.

Impressed with their display of loyalty and fearful of pushing them too far, too soon, Peter Sion waved his hand and Oscar let go the wheel of William's stretching.

"Well done, men. You may take your well-deserved rest."

Sion stood before the gasping Jonathan. He admired the rapid in and out movement of his abdominal wall, as Jonathan filled his lungs with oxygen to replenish his spent muscles. Even in a relaxed state of full suspension, this man's abdomen reeked of sheer power. The entire body exclaimed it, made louder by the shimmering of manly sweat. Again, Sion felt the hardness of Jonathan's belly with clutching fingertips.

"Never give an inch. Is that it, Mr. Sikes?"

"Why... why are you doing this? We've done nothing... you... know this."

"I know nothing, other than what I see. And what I see fascinates me. Your torture does not begin until your Bishop is here to listen. Then, it is serious. For now, it is a softening."

Jonathan dropped his chin to rest on his chest. He locked eyes with those of his tormentor, not to express anger, but to elicit sympathy between heavy breaths. "If I am the one you want... then... please... let William go."

"I cannot do that."

"Please, sire... why must he suffer? Take me... do as you will... but... don't torture William... I... I cannot bear to see it."

"I want you both, but for different reasons."

Sion turned away from Jonathan and journeyed to the Steps, ignoring the very angry cries coming from the Board of Impalement.

"God almighty! What... kind of man are you? Have you... no heart? Touch him again and I... I will..." Jonathan collapsed in surrender, abandoning his thought. He did not know what it would take to incur the full wrath of Peter Sion, but he wisely realized that this was no time to be testing those limits.

Sion sat on the step level with William's chest and placed an open hand onto sweat-drenched hair. He touched William's sternum with his fingertip, then drew a line through his perspiration from chest to belly button.

"You are a strong one, William. There is no doubt."

"What do you want from us? What can we say to make you stop?"

"Nothing. Not to me. I want to test your strength. That is all."

"But, why? We've done nothing to harm you. We have always been loyal to you."

"I know this, William. You hear rumors. You fear what you have heard. You fear that you will leave this room a broken man, but I can assure you that this is not the case."

"Then, what is it? What do you want?"

"You will know soon enough."

Part Six - Dedicated to Serve

One member of Peter Sion's entourage had not participated in the test of loyalty perpetrated upon Jonathan and William, and that was Otto. He had been busy with another project. Otto's activity came as a result of loyalty proven long ago – his loyalty to Peter Sion.

Otto stood at the hearth of an open fireplace built into the wall a few feet to the left of William's stretch rack. Above the burning embers hung a black kettle, and in this kettle was a green, gooey liquid, a concoction brewed by Sion, who fancied himself to be some sort of wizard.

Over the years, Peter Sion had become well-versed in the dark arts of magic, beginning with the day he summoned an aging, well-respected sorceress from the hinterlands. After tempting her with the security of an official residence in his castle, he studied with her, learning everything contained in her book of medicines, as well as the knowledge stored in her head. Her residence and her life in Egbert Castle lasted for nearly two years, until Sion was just as skilled as she, and upon her death, he properly built a monument to her outside his bedroom window. Looking down to a grass-covered, open-air and private courtyard inside the castle walls, Sion would and still did every morning pay homage to her burial ground. He did this out of respect. He also did it as a precaution, lest he anger her spirit and invite a rash of her evil spells upon him, a battle of which he did not care to provoke.

One battle that had been forced upon Peter Sion seemed trifling in its beginning; then it became an annoyance; then it became a serious threat that nearly cost him his life.

Thieves had struck, the attack reportedly to have occurred on a lonely road connecting settlements in Sion's realm, with some hapless farmer as victim. When first told of the incident, Peter dispatched patrols of soldiers to find the bandits, expecting any day to see them brought before him in bondage or as corpses.

But it was not to be. These men were clever, somehow always eluding Sion's patrols. As days and weeks passed with more robberies and still no results, Sion's frustration grew to the extent that he decided to solve the problem himself. He summoned his trusted henchmen.

"Men, we will go on the hunt. We will track down these weasels and bring them to justice."

Oscar and Herman enthusiastically welcomed a change in their routine, but Otto was a bit uneasy.

"Do we know their number?"

"We have reports of three, four, five and six. You know these scatter-brained peasants cannot be relied upon for accurate witness."

Otto rubbed his chin. "We are four."

"And we are soldiers," Sion boasted. "Surely we can outwit common thieves, regardless of their number."

The men dressed not as soldiers, but as commoners with wool trousers tucked into leather riding boots, wool shirts beneath roughened-leather jackets. On horseback, they traveled to the scene of the most recent attack, a stretch of road cleared through forest growth far removed from the nearest traces of human existence.

"They entered here." Otto found a trail of hooves leaving the road and entering the forest.

"How many?" Sion asked.

"I expect four men."

"How long since they passed through here?"

"Two, perhaps three hours."

"They will stop to count their booty. Let's move."

With Otto in the lead, they followed the broken-limbed swath left by the bandits, as Otto confirmed the trail of horse hooves when he saw them. The terrain became difficult, a steep hill to their right forcing them to constantly lean that direction, as their horses traversed a slow, sideways grade. Suddenly, a rustling from above caused all four men to look to their right. A quartet of huge, rounded stones tumbled down the hill not more than 40 feet above them. The deafening cracks of boulders crashing against sturdy tree trunks echoed through the forest, and although each collision caused the stones to change direction left and right, nothing could alter their threatening direction down the hill towards Sion and his men.

The men scattered and prayed, for no direction was safe. Otto bolted forward and Sion followed him, while Herman and Oscar turned back and graded down the hill. Their decision was not sound, as their horses could not navigate the rough, downhill grade at speed. They tumbled, throwing both men past their steeds and to the ground. Oscar's horse followed him In its fall, coming to rest atop his legs, where it struggled to its feet despite having broken its leg. For good measure, Oscar's horse, in its attempt to rise, cracked Oscar's thigh bone in the process.

Meanwhile, Herman's horse continued rolling well clear of him. Other than a few cuts and scrapes, Herman was unharmed, as he lay on his belly in thick undergrowth. But then the crashing of boulder to wood caused him to look up the hill. One of the boulders was no more than ten feet above him. He sprang to his hands and knees, crawling to his left out of its path, only to have the boulder clip another tree and roll directly in front of him. As it passed, it rolled across Herman's left arm before continuing its rapid path of destruction downhill, terrorizing and chasing his horse along the way. He knew before trying to lift it that his forearm had been crushed, as was his left hand, and although Herman's injury was not near the severity of Oscar's, the pain was.

As for the other two, Otto had wisely kept his horse at speed on level grade, with Sion close behind. Their direction and pace should have taken them from danger, but one stone seemed to have eyes of destruction. It clipped one tree after another, always changing its course to plot a direct path where Otto and Peter were soon to be. Even so, Peter's horse was nearly clear when the boulder reached them, until the massive sphere traversed over a slab of rock jutting from the ground. This slab acted as a ramp, launching the boulder into the air to violently crash against Peter's shoulder. With an incredible, devastating velocity it sent Peter flying from his horse. He landed nearly twenty feet from where he had ridden and continued to roll another twenty before coming to a sudden stop, courtesy of the unmovable trunk of a tree.

When the sound of tumbling boulder changed from Otto's right ear to his left, he halted his horse and watched Peter's riderless steed streak past him in terror. He quickly turned back to search for his leader, looking down the hill where the tumbling boulder could still be seen and heard smashing into sturdy tree trunks.

Otto's eyes scanned back from the boulder until the form of Peter Sion was spotted, motionless, laying near one of the trees. He dismounted and traversed down the steep hill, his heart sinking with each step. It was not good. Otto knelt beside a face-down man whose left rib cage was curved in alignment with and pressed against the tree. His left arm was beyond his head and bent in a direction it should not go. His right arm laid beside him with a curve to its upper portion that should not have been. He was breathing, but unresponsive, and while the outer damage appeared bad enough, Peter's inner damage could possibly be worse. This unknown filled Otto with dread, but hearing men behind him brought some relief.

Otto assumed the voices coming from up the hill were those of Oscar and Herman, but when he turned to look, four men were waving at him as they led his horse away. Good fortune was bestowed to the bandits that day – or bad fortune for Oscar, Herman and Peter, depending on perspective. In less than thirty seconds, a low-percentage-for-success, hit-or-miss launching of downhill boulders had incapacitated three out of four men. Now, the predicament had worsened. Otto was afoot with a gravely injured man, while Oscar and Herman were nowhere in sight. Otto knew he must find them. He had to know their fate before he could know his own.

He called to them with powerful lungs, but heard nothing. He returned to the path he and Sion had taken in their flight and called from there. The distant voice of Herman answered his call.

"Where are your horses?" Otto shouted, with hands cuffed to mouth.

"One is lame, the other gone." Herman answered. "And yours?"

"One gone... one taken."

"By them?"

"Yes."

"Did you see them?"

Otto was not concerned with them, needing instead to preserve his voice for yelling out what was important. "Peter is injured... very bad."

"We both are injured."

"Can you walk?"

"Yes... Oscar, no."

"The farm house... I will meet you there."

It was the last semblance of civilization they had seen before entering the forest. Herman and Oscar would have to fend for themselves, because Otto's only concern was for Peter Sion. He scanned in all directions in hoping that one of the horses might have returned, but saw none. No horses meant no supplies and no weapons, other than the hunting knife he kept pouched and strapped to his hip. All actions taken would be by hand and foot.

Returning down the hill to Peter's tree, Otto saw that the circumstances had not changed better or worse. A decision had to be made. While it was true that moving the man might further damage him or end his life altogether, it was also true that leaving him and running for help would put him in grave danger. Darkness would fall before Otto could return, which would make it nearly impossible to find the damn tree. Bandits were about. Wild beasts were about, and Otto's decision was made for him. He would not leave his king to lie on the ground alone.

Otto set about to undergo an amazing test of human dedication and endurance. He found a massive, but dying tree with splitting bark and broke off pieces to make a splint. Otto could not break the bark willy-nilly, for he needed his pieces to be of a certain width and length. Removing the six-inch blade from his hip pouch, he carved straight lines along the thick-barked tree trunk. Next, he followed the lines with thumbs and fingers to bend and break on his carved lines. It was a tedious process and required great strength. It resulted in broken fingernails and bloody fingertips, but Otto got his splints.

He searched the forest for vines, but found none. Instead, he would use tree roots to bind the splints. He dug into the earth with knife and already damaged fingers until he found long lines of tributary roots in small diameters he could use. Digging with knife and pulling upwards with his gripped fingers, he exposed the lengths needed to make ties. He severed them with his knife and Otto got his six sections of root.

Returning to Peter, he delicately shifted his subject's body away from the tree trunk. He laid one of his splints with the inside curve facing upwards, and then cris-crossed three pairs of roots beneath the splint, leaving opposing ends exposed on either side of the splint. He gingerly lifted Peter with arms beneath his torso and shifted him to lay face up in the nestling curvature of the splint. After placing the second splint to rest upon Peter's chest, its inside curve cradling him, Otto straddled both splints with his feet and pulled each pair of roots upwards, cris-crossing them again and knotting them tightly together. One pair of roots bound the splints near Peter's shoulders; one pair crossed at his abdomen; and one crossed at mid-thigh.

Otto inspected his work. The two splints were separated by two inches outside of Peter's arms. The curves of the bark were outside with Peter resting inside, as though encased by the trunk of a fallen tree. The top edges of the splints were even with the top of Peter's head and the lower edges midway on his calves, so that only his ankles and feet were exposed. The pressure held Peter secure without crushing him and his breathing, although shallow, was rhythmically steady. It was time for Otto to bear his load, the riskiest phase of his endeavor.

He faced the head end of his construct and lifted it just enough so that its lower edge and Peter's heels were in contact with the ground. With an upward thrust, he launched its weight into the air a few inches, released his grasp and quickly turned 180 degrees. In the split second Peter and the splints were suspended in mid-air, Otto bent at the waist and positioned himself beneath the construct, which came crashing onto his spine with him in a squatted position. He immediately reached up with both arms and grasped onto both edges of the lower splint on either side of Peter's shoulders.

Otto's feet were spread wide, flat on the ground with his legs scrunched into a squat. The upper section of the lower splint ran the length of his back, as both hands clutched tightly to its edges. He maneuvered himself backwards, pivoting on the balls of his feet to shift his position by fractions of inches, until he felt comfortable with the length of splint under his control. Then, with a mighty burst of strength from his arms, calves and thighs, Otto tilted the construct and Peter, lifting them to a perfectly horizontal level, supported below by the length of his back.

Inside the splint, the back of Peter's head rested directly above the back of Otto's head. Otto's waist was bent to 90 degrees, as his mighty legs held the king aloft and his powerful arms bore the weight of extended splint beyond his own buttocks. It was time for their journey to begin.

Otto climbed the hill and returned to the path. He retraced their horse-hoof steps with his human steps, until they reached the road that led to a farm house that led to a wagon-ride to Egbert Castle.

It was Peter Sion's good fortune that Otto was his savior, because the journey from tree trunk to farm house was sixteen miles. Each splint weighed nearly twenty pounds, while the man inside weighed one hundred seventy-six. It is true that Otto could have attempted his task by using only the lower splint, but to him, this would not suffice. Otto expected that he would encounter obstacles and fatigue that might cause him to lose control of his load, and if such an event were to occur, Peter's chances of surviving would be increased with a total encasement. Otto also knew that briars and thorns would line his path, and his king was not to be exposed to such elements.

Every step taken was with Otto's back perfectly horizontal beneath Peter's splinted back. The steps were taken on an inclined trail, over dirt, moss, tree roots and stones, through thick brush, through hanging branches and through ice-cold streams. The pressure on Otto's ankles and his feet was a constant of weight bearing down from above and incline pushing from his left. The outward curvature of the hard splint pressed directly onto his spine, wood against bone, bruising him with every step. His bloodied fingers and thumbs were forced to maintain constant pressure on the splint in order to keep his patient steady and horizontal. His lower back, hips, thighs and calves were required to absorb every shock of every step in order to keep from jolting his patient's damaged ribs and broken bones. With the end portion of splint resting on the back of his head, Otto's eyes could view no more than five feet in front of him, and that was with eyeballs strained to remain lifted to the upper reaches of their sockets.

And there was no rest. Otto knew that lowering and raising his king would risk further injury to him. He also knew that once he lowered the combined weight of man and two pieces of heavy wood from his back he would never have the strength to raise them again. And so, Otto trudged onward. For sixteen agonizing miles he continued. It was a feat of strength and endurance beyond human possibility, but he did it.

It was his duty as a soldier. He did it for love of his king, of Peter Sion.

Otto's dedication did not end with their arrival to Egbert Castle. It should have, but Otto would have none of it. He assisted with the removal of clothing and hovered nearby as the medical examination took place. He assisted with the washing of Sion's body and scrutinized the wrapping of his rib cage. His watchful eye inspected the splints placed on Peter's left arm and right arm and the bandages wrapped around his head. Otto declined medical treatment for himself, and when all that could be done for Peter had been done, and Bishop Frederick Bethune and all attendants had exited the room, Otto instructed the guards standing outside that no one was to enter without his permission. He locked the door and collapsed onto the bed. Otto laid on his side facing his king, crossways, between the foot of the mattress and the covered feet of Peter.

Nine hours passed before Otto heard a voice – a weakened voice that repeatedly mumbled but one word. "Otto."

Otto had been Peter's last conscious memory before that boulder smashed into him. The image of Otto riding swiftly ahead of him is what awakened Peter Sion, and not knowing where he was or who was present, he called out for the man who had so desperately tried to save them both. Otto stood at bedside and took Peter's hand. He told the story, some of it heard and some of it not, as Peter drifted in and out of consciousness. It was a beginning. The king was safe. Peter's healing had begun.

Other than the purveyors of medicine, Otto barred everyone from Peter Sion's bedroom. Even his cousin Herman and brother Oscar were barred, they having reached the farm house *after* Otto and Peter were on their way to the castle.

One other exception was Frederick Bethune, who requested he be allowed to meditate for his friend's recovery.

"Five minutes," Otto barked.

Bethune did not argue. He knelt beside the bed and prayed silently, with Peter sleeping peacefully in the center of the mattress.

The soldier in Otto interrupted Bethune when his time was up. Not one extra second was given.

Again, Bethune did not argue, but he did make a suggestion. "Otto, the servants of this castle are here for a reason. They know better how to care..."

"They are not to be trusted. Nor are you. You may have five minutes per day. That is all."

"Damn you," the Bishop's temper was very un-Bishop-like. "Who do you think you are? What gives you the right..."

"Frederick." Peter spoke softly, having been awakened by the Bishop speaking loudly. "Otto knows what is best. Do as he says. Please"

Bishop Bethune softened his heart, remembering that this man had saved the life of his king. "Forgive me, Otto." He placed a kiss to Otto's forehead. "It is your right to see this through."

Throughout Peter Sion's recovery, meals were placed outside the door for Otto to retrieve. All food and drink was given to Peter by Otto. All bedpans for urine and feces were handled by Otto. All washing of the body, cleaning of the mouth, shaving of the beard and trimming of the nails was done by Otto.

Not until Peter was on his feet and completely independent did Otto leave his master's bedroom, and that was at the suggestion of Peter himself.

They exited Peter's living quarters and made their way to the dungeon, where Otto visited with Herman and Oscar for the first time since the incident. Their journey to safety had also been remarkable, but paling in comparison to Otto's. With splints built for Oscar's broken leg and Herman's broken arm, Herman's good arm had supported Oscar, as they hobbled through the rough terrain leading back to the road. There, they were rescued by the wife of the farmer who had long ago departed for Egbert Castle with Otto and Peter in his wagon.

The four of them compared scars, while Otto mocked them for their inferiority.

"At least you had supplies carried by the lame horse. You both could walk, at least with three legs, yet Peter and I arrived long before you two. You are weak. I have known this all along."

"He is correct, you know," Peter seconded. "Thank god I followed Otto and not you two."

Herman and Oscar did not argue. They had no argument to support them.

"Come, all of you," Peter invited. "I must see my beloved instruments of interrogation. I have missed them so."

Four together journeyed to the torture chamber. Once there, Peter Sion issued an order in a tone not friendly.

"Herman, Oscar, strip him." Sion pointed to Otto, who was stunned by this command. He stood with mouth agape, but did not resist them, nor did he speak words of protest. Sworn to serve – duty and dedication – Otto held firm to his beliefs.

"Not his loin cloth. It stays." Sion supervised the process of Otto's exposure and humiliation, then chose the implement of choice. "Put him on the table."

They took Otto by his arms for escort, but he cast them aside. "I do not need their assistance. Allow me the dignity of facing my torture like a man, if my torture is your aim."

Otto proudly walked between them to the round, horizontal table, climbed onto its surface and laid on his back. Grasping Otto's right wrist, Herman pulled his arm towards the corresponding mount beyond and to the right of Otto's head, while Oscar did the same with his left arm. They roped his wrists and turned the cranks on each mount, stretching both arms taut to form the letter V. This process was repeated on his ankles and legs, leaving Otto stretched to form the letter X.

"Leave us."

Oscar and Herman exited the room as Sion locked the door behind them. He slowly circled the table to inspect his prisoner, taking in his muscular strength from every angle.

Of course, the question repeated itself in Otto's mind. His torment could not be stifled, and with only himself and his king in the room, Otto dared to ask. He did so in a soldierly manner of respect.

"Why must I be tortured, sire?"

"Shhh..." Sion climbed onto the table and knelt beside the man's mighty chest. He pressed a finger to his lips. "Do not question. Do not speak. Close your eyes and accept your fate."

No command could have been more difficult for Otto to obey. How could he possibly remain silent? With such treachery perpetrated against him, how could he not cry out in anguish? What had he done? How had he failed? Did he not have the right to know?

As Sion stepped down from the table, Otto closed his eyes and prepared for the worst, remaining loyal to the wishes of his king.

"So, this is the foot that brought me to safety." Sion laid his nails onto the ball of Otto's left foot. He scraped the sole with a light touch, drawing four lines down the arch and to the heel, as Otto curled his toes forward in a defensive response.

Peter removed his nails. He turned the crank one revolution, increasing the tension on Otto's left leg a few inches more. Moving midway between both legs, he stood at table's edge and viewed his obedient soldier. As asked, Otto's eyes and lips were closed. He did not struggle against his ropes. He was stretched, but as of yet not painfully so. Still, the tension caused his chest to expand and abdomen to flatten. From the foot-view, his nipple tips rose above his dark chest hair. A dark, thick line of hair dropped from his sternum, following the downward-sloping muscle of his abdomen. It continued to his stretched navel, entering and exiting, where below it widened its path before disappearing beneath Otto's loin cloth. Peter Sion stripped down to his loin cloth.

"And this one..." He wrapped the fingers of his right hand over the top of Otto's right foot, using his thumb to massage the ball, arch and heel. "How many steps? How many torturous steps were taken?" Using his left hand, Peter pushed back the toes, opening the arch for his lips to touch. "Mmm, I can taste their power." He worshiped the arch with the tip of his tongue. "How can I repay them... these hard-working feet... these beautiful... thick... sturdy... hard-working... manly feet?"

Peter turned the crank to further tighten the right leg, and then he launched a full assault upon Otto's right foot. He bent back the toes and painted its arch and heel with saliva-thick strokes of his tongue, verbalizing between his praise. "How can I thank them enough?" He separated the toes with his fingers, working his tongue between them. "The feet that carried me." He sucked each toe with lips and tongue. "The feet that sacrificed themselves for me."

He leapt onto the table and assaulted the left shin, licking and kissing the muscular calves on either side, while tugging the lengthy dark hairs with his lips. "And these powerful legs. They did their part, too." He transferred his praise to the right shin and attacked with fury. "What should I say?" He worked on the knee and thigh, first the right and then the left. "What can I do? How can I repay these manly feet... these massive, fur-covered legs?"

Peter knelt between Otto's thighs and formed two fists with two hands. He leaned forward to plant both of those fists to the heart of Otto's belly, using the solid wall to support his weight.

"By worshiping you, Otto, that is how." Peter removed his fists and buried his face into Otto's belly. He licked and kissed its hard, flattened surface. He darkened its already dark hairs with his spit and traced the oval rim of the belly button with the tip of his tongue. Peter followed the thick line of fur onto the pit of Otto's stomach, using his tongue to moisten its masculine beauty. Then, he removed his mouth, and with his hands planted to the table's surface on either side of Otto's rib cage, Peter Sion issued another command. "Look at me."

Otto opened his eyes, raised his head and peered over his chest. Otto's eyes were moist.

"No man could do what you did, Otto. You *are* a bull... *my* little bull." He leaned down and pecked Otto's sternum with a kiss. "Nothing can defeat you." He pressed his face onto Otto's thick-furred chest and rubbed left to right. "No man can approach you." He sat on Otto's chest with knees straddling him. "I will praise my little bull." He supported the back of Otto's head with his hand and placed a kiss onto Otto's forehead. "I will lay you upon a pedestal... *my* pedestal... and worship you for the rest of my life." He peppered Otto's forehead, nose, cheeks and lips with kisses. "My little bull... the man who saved my life."

What happened next was perhaps the most intense body worship every perpetrated upon a man. Otto lowered his head to the table, closed his eyes and basked in this praise, while Peter assaulted him with lips, tongue, fingers and hands. No part of his little bull was neglected. Every inch of top-side skin was traversed, from the tips of his toes to the tips of his fingers. And when the time came to praise the pinnacle of this man's strength – when the cloth was removed to reveal this man's glorious phallus, a manly organ equal in strength to the man himself – Otto obeyed his commander's wishes once again. Otto joyously surrendered his seed. Otto, ever the loyal soldier, Peter's little bull, performed his duty to his king with an explosion capable of inseminating an entire herd.

From that day forward, Otto remained on Peter Sion's pedestal. From that day forward, Otto and Peter were no longer soldier and king. They were partners for life.

Tank Books

Part Seven - Helena's Folly

Although William did not care to have Peter Sion's finger playing with his belly button, he did enjoy the respite from being stretched on the rack.

To his left, Otto stood near the fireplace. With a long, wooden pole, he stirred the slowly-warming mixture, as Sion descended the steps and joined him to inspect.

"Look, little bull, it is almost ready. Soon the steam will rise, then we will see if this man can live up to his reputation."

He took the pole from Otto and stirred for himself. "Yes, just the right temperature and thickness." Peter cast the stirring pole aside and turned to his partner. "Otto, it is time to challenge William Corder's manhood."

Suddenly, Frederick Bethune entered the torture chamber, dressed as though for mass in the full regalia of his Bishop attire. "Peter, we have a visitor."

"Who?"

"Her name is Helena Sikes." Bethune stood inches from the twisted face of the hapless William. He scanned up and down the elongated form with eyes squinting. "You know, Peter, these two are the finest men we have yet plucked from the village."

"It is true, Frederick. I have been gentle with them in hopes you would join us."

"I appreciate that, but church matters have interfered."

"What does this woman want?"

"I do not know. I was told she has a request of me, but the gist of it..."

"Tell her what's happening here," William interrupted. "Tell her to say the truth."

Bethune ordered Oscar to, "Rack him," and it was done. Then, he addressed the groaning man. "I will tell her nothing. It is not your concern. Save yourself, William Corder."

"I... am... innocent."

"Nobody is innocent, you foolish man." He nodded to Oscar, who released the spoke to stop William's stretching. Turning to Sion, the Bishop prodded. "Come, Peter, we will hear this woman's request."

"But my potion is ready."

"It can wait. These men are going nowhere."

Reluctantly, Sion made arrangements to join the Bishop. "Men, do nothing until you hear from me. Give them water and leave them to rest, but do not allow them to speak to one another."

Bishop Bethune and Peter Sion traversed the long corridor leading to an up stairwell, conversing along the way.

"Peter, it is true what they said of the woman."

"How do you know this?"

"She has come for her lover, Tobias."

"He is here?"

"Yes. Our spies saw the woman tempt him. Once his blacksmith duties were finished he went to her house. They were bedded when the soldiers arrested him."

"So, she has come to plead for his life."

"Of course, and in the process will condemn herself. I thought you might enjoy the scene."

"Indeed I will, Frederick."

As they entered the inquisition chamber, Sion schemed for a way to monitor the activities in his playroom, while still delighting in the useless pleadings of a heartbroken woman. He softly muttered an incantation of wizardry. Within seconds, his inner, spiritual form – the form composed of ether that leaves us when we dream – separated and drifted from his outer, physical form. Sion's subconsciousness floated away from the inquisition chamber and down the corridor leading back to the dungeons. His consciousness and his physical body remained with Bethune, fully functional, and both men assumed their positions on the stone benches. The Bishop gave his order to the standing-guard soldiers. "We will now hear the request of Helena Sikes. Bring her."

On the wall above the open fireplace, where hung the black kettle full of Sion's bubbling liquid potion, in the room containing two bound men, a face appeared and a voice was heard. The apparition was seen and heard only by one – Otto. The voice made a suggestion to him. "Otto, conceal the eyes of Jonathan Sikes and begin the treatment to William Corder. You know where."

Otto recognized the faint image of Peter Sion and did as he was told. In a trance-like state, he grabbed one of the ladders stacked in the corner and climbed to tie a blindfold around the head of Jonathan Sikes, while Oscar and Herman sat resting to Otto's right on the horizontal table. They were unconcerned with Otto's activities. They had seen him this way before. Otto long ago had assumed the position of Sion's closest assistant in the torture chamber and elsewhere. Although they did not understand how or why these things happened to him, neither Herman nor Oscar ever interfered with Otto's activities or questioned Sion's motives. Experience had shown them that whatever might happen was merely a part of the interrogation. None of these spells had ever caused harm to Otto, and so their trust of and loyalty to Peter Sion remained firm.

Using a long-handled ladle, Otto scooped a portion of the green liquid from the black kettle, and then moved towards William. His body tensed when he saw the steam rising from the ladle and he struggled with all strength to break his bonds. A gallant effort it was, but useless.

"What... what is that? No, please... not that... not there..."

Otto slowly poured the concoction onto the testicles and penis of William Corder, then stood back to watch the potion take effect. Howls of agony and shock echoed through the room, as William endured a hot-liquid assault upon his genitals.

"William, what is it?" Jonathan violently struggled to break free. The tone of his friend's agonized voice was not the same as before. It was an unknown expression unlike any heard during William's stretching, and this filled Jonathan with both rage and fear. The not knowing of what was happening became more painful to him than any physical torture to his own body could. "For God's sakes... what are they doing to you?"

Cries of anguish were the only sounds coming from the mouth of William. He also was consumed with fear – his own fear of not knowing. Gravity caused the thick fluid to creep along the exposed topside of his shaft, soon encompassing his phallus, testicles and scrotum in searing heat. How could he know what damage was being done to his manhood? What would be left of him? What would be the use of living if his manhood was taken from him? This is what struck fear into the soul of William. It was a fear so great that he did not hear the pleadings of his friend Jonathan, and therefore, he did not answer. He continued to scream while fighting back his tears.

Peter Sion's apparition was pleased.

In the Chamber of Inquisition, Helena Sikes was brought by two soldiers and held standing before Bethune and Sion. She had chosen her favorite attire for this visit, or at least it was her favorite attire for when she wished to appear pious, wholesome and virtuous – a white dress of length to conceal all of her, except for her ankles, shoes, hands, neck, face, head and hair. She stood with head bowed in reverence, as Bishop Bethune addressed her. "Woman, state your business."

"Your Holiness, soldiers have arrested Tobias Corder. Do you know of this?"

"No, I do not. Peter, do you know of this?"

"Yes, I do. He was taken from the bed of a married woman."

"Oh, I see. That is a very serious offense. Of what interest is this man to you, Helena Sikes?"

"He is, um..." The treacherous fool was stopped cold, as she suddenly realized her coming here was a serious blunder. "Tobias is, uh, so young and innocent. Surely he can be forgiven for one mistake."

On the Steps to Purgatory, the green goo began to cool and thicken, and so did the penis of William Corder. The horrific pain of searing heat subsided. It was replaced by a comforting, stimulating heat which caused his organ to fill with blood. Despite his best mental efforts to prevent it, William's cock ballooned in both width and length. Its inflation caused it to rise and separate itself from his testicles. Gravity did the rest. William's penis flipped onto his belly, stretching towards his navel and slithering along his downward sloping trail of belly fur.

"Otto," came the voice from above. "Another layer."

In a repeat of the application, more green liquid came from Otto's ladle, coating testicles and cock to intensify William's stimulation. Although fresh from the kettle, this coating did not burn painfully, because the first layer protected him from its agonizing heat. William's screams were no more. He became silent, as an eerie calm and sense of well-being allayed his fears.

Jonathan also became quiet, but his fears were intensified. Hearing nothing from William, his only hope was that the poor man had lost consciousness. This is the thought to which he focused, for the alternative was unthinkable. For all Jonathan knew, William's silence could also mean his life was no more, and this was a thought too horrid for the blindfolded man to bear.

From his stone bench, Bishop Bethune looked at Sion, smiled and turned the screw on his female visitor. "I am confused, my dear. Are you not the one who accused William Corder of raping you?"

"Yes, Father."

"Is this man Tobias not his younger brother?"

"He is."

"Then, why do you plead for the mercy of one, while condemning the other?"

Silence befell the Chamber of Inquisition. There was no answer she could give without condemning herself.

Sion's laughter broke the silence, as Bethune taunted this pea-brained female. He turned to his partner with a question. "Peter, did your soldiers give the name of this married woman, the one violated by Tobias Corder?"

"Yes, Frederick. I believe her name was Sikes... Helena Sikes."

"What is this?" Bishop Bethune bellowed and rose from his bench for dramatic effect. "Tell me, my dear, are you not that very same

Helena Sikes?"

With eyes cast to the floor, she spoke softly. "Yes, Father."

"So, both Corders raped you. Is that it? First William, then Tobias. Is this correct?"

Hopelessly trapped, the foolish woman had to make a quick decision. She could either lie yet again to save herself, or tell the truth in an attempt to save Tobias.

"Speak up, woman." Bishop Bethune mocked her with arms outstretched and palms open to symbolize his feigned confusion. "I am waiting. What is your answer?"

"No, Father, I cannot tell you."

He sat on the bench, bringing his fingertips to touch one another and form a triangle, striking an image of pious superiority. "What can you not tell me? Tobias Corder was dragged from your bed. Did he not also rape you?"

Peter Sion and Bishop Bethune sat waiting for the wretched woman to admit her foul deeds, but Peter Sion sat with a full erection hidden beneath his clothing. He quickly was losing interest in the charade being played with Helena Sikes, desiring instead to join Otto in the torment of William Corder. The sight of this vicious female, who now had fallen to her knees in tears, sickened him beyond description and he expressed it to her with a shout that nearly caused the walls to crumble.

"Out with it, you evil wench. Two men have suffered because of you, soon to be three. Tell the truth to your Bishop Bethune. He is a reasonable man. Maybe he will show mercy. Maybe he will not. But speak now, or I myself will beat it out of you."

"No, please, it is a lie."

"What is a lie, my dear?" Bethune intensified the pressure. "That William Corder raped you, or that Tobias Corder did not?"

Five seconds of moaning sobs were all that Peter Sion would allow. "Frederick, there is no hope for her."

"It is true. She is evil through and through. By telling me these vicious untruths, she also deceives the Pope and Our Heavenly Father. She cannot be saved."

"Helena Sikes," Bishop Bethune turned to pass judgement on the woman. "I sentence you to hang by your wrists until you rot. May God have mercy on your wretched soul."

As she collapsed to lie face down on the floor, now flooding it with very real tears, Peter Sion interjected. "Before you have her strung up, I think she should be forced to see the result of her treachery. Let her see what has happened to William Corder and Jonathan Sikes. Perhaps she would like to entertain her husband. Maybe if she had given more of herself to him in the first place, none of this would have happened."

Bethune smiled. "You are correct, but I dare say things have worked out rather well for us."

"Better than we could have imagined, Frederick."

Part Eight - For Love of Suffering

Peter Sion summoned his spiritual self to rejoin the physical, and then he and Frederick Bethune followed the guards as they dragged the screaming and sobbing Helena Sikes from the Chamber of Inquisition. In the corridor, Bethune placed his hand upon Sion's shoulder.

"Peter, I will join this spectacle soon enough, but first, I think it best I prepare the necessary paperwork for dispatch to Rome."

"Can that not wait, Frederick? You have yet to fully enjoy these glorious men. I cannot describe for you the extent of their beauty – so helplessly stretched and vulnerable. Don't you care to see their reaction when I present Helena Sikes to them?"

"No, not now. We want no loopholes in the execution of this woman. Everything must be in order. It is for our own protection."

Sion did not press further with the issue. He had made his offer to share, but his mind was focused on the scene awaiting him. His anxiety was nearly uncontrollable, knowing that the amazing cock and balls of William Corder were in full force and yearning. With no more words to say, Sion followed the guards and Helena Sikes to the dungeon, while Bethune went another direction.

He climbed the stairwell to the Grand Hall, a spacious room that centered the castle. All corridors and stairwells converged upon this room. Frederick continued up another set of stairs which led to the section of Egbert Castle devoted to him. The circular staircase came to the floor of a hallway, where two guards stood sentry. To

Bethune's left, two doors, one which opened to his administrative office and one that concealed his living space. To his right, a set of double doors, behind which lay a private chapel built specifically for the Bishop of Grunewald, whoever that might happen to be at the time.

The father of Peter Sion had ordered the building of this chapel as a way to further consecrate his union with the Holy Roman Church and blessing of the Pope. For the past 22 years, this had been Frederick Bethune's private sanctuary, a place where he was not to be disturbed for any reason by any person other than Peter Sion, and only then if the Bishop's life might be in some sort of imminent danger.

Upon opening the doors, he was greeted by fading daylight filtering through tall, cathedral-arched windows of leaded glass. Their expanse began eight feet above the floor and majestically curved upwards another seventeen, coming to points just below the ceiling. Shadows of early-evening blue darkened the white walls, made darker by the handsome, cherry wood trimmings that framed windows and doors to match the inlaid, cherry wood floor.

The view to his right included the windows, a slightly raised marble platform where sat an alter also made of marble, along with two, high-backed cherry wood chairs flanking the alter and facing towards the glass openings beyond. To his left were columned pedestals, six of them in a line that were also of marble and rose from the floor to waist level. Upon these pedestals would rest six bronze busts representing six previous Popes of the Roman Church. Beyond the pedestals near the curved wall were two metal stands supporting two heavy candles, both lit to provide illumination for the columned busts.

Frederick Bethune turned to his left, where he saw not the six Popes – for he had removed their busts – but instead, upon one of the two centered and columned platforms, he saw Tobias Corder. The young man was draped atop the pedestal with ankles and wrists bound. His buttocks rested on the pedestal, while the remainder of his form was suspended in air, gravity pulling him towards the floor. Chains bolted to the floor rose in four lines, connecting to iron cuffs locked onto his four limbs. His spine was torturously arched backwards, as the chains pulled his arms straight and far apart, angling diagonally towards the floor on one side of the column, while his knees were bent, chains pulling his feet down on the other side of the column.

Tobias gasped for air. His diaphragm was brutally compressed. Only the pedestal beneath his muscular buttocks kept him aloft, while the rest of his body was left hanging on all sides. And what was the pinnacle of this horrendous curve? The organs of sex, covered by his only protective clothing. Inside a tantalizing, bulging pouch, decked in the official royal blue color of Egbert Castle, the amazing penis and testicles of Tobias Corder lay hidden, while the remainder of his skin lay bare. His youthfully muscled body struggled against the chains that bound him.

"Father... why?" Tobias gasped between shortened intakes of air. "Why... are you... doing this to me?"

"Do not fret, Tobias." Bishop Bethune inspected his prize, circling between the columns, his eyes inhaling the glorious beauty of stretched muscle and smooth skin. "No harm will come to you, for you are under my protection." He removed his Bishop's hat and laid it atop an empty pedestal. "You are too young to understand the dangers of this world, but I will teach you." He unbuttoned the inner lining of his ceremonial robe from neck to navel, fondling his own chest and nipples. "You were nearly ruined by that evil wench, Helena Sikes, but you have been rescued just in time."

"No, Father," Tobias pleaded. "Please... is that... why I am here? It was... not my fault... She tempted me... I was..."

"Shush, Tobias." Bethune placed a finger to the man's lips. "You are innocent. I know this." His fingertip left a trail from the lower lip to the chin. Bethune pressed his thumb to the young man's cheek and gently rubbed four fingers along the skin of his neck.

"You must trust your Bishop, Tobias." With open hand, Bethune felt the bushy growth along his subject's stretched-open armpit, sliding his fingers onto the man's pectoral. He gently squeezed the powerful muscle, while rubbing his thumb across the elongated nipple. He watched with excitement as his touch brought stimulation to the stretched orb, causing its skin to contract and tip to rise.

"Remain loyal to me, and you will never need fear again." He slid his hand to the other pectoral, repeating his stimulation to that nipple. His trail continued along the sternum, onto the flattened and stretched stomach. He formed a claw and lightly pressed into the hard wall of muscle. The abdominal wall rose and fell at a rapid pace and each movement dramatically outlined every detail of every muscle between sternum and pelvic bone. Bethune marveled at its beauty, his flattened hand massaging its entire surface. A fine trail of light hair sprouted from the navel, thickening and darkening as it moved towards the loin cloth, widening before disappearing beneath.

"Please... Father," Tobias moaned. "I... I am in pain"

"I know, my son."

"I... cannot breathe."

"You are strong, Tobias."

"Why... why do you... torture me?"

"I do not torture you, my innocent one. You must suffer... for me... for yourself. Only then will you be cleansed. The female has soiled you, but I will heal you."

Tobias gasped for air. Only the powerful muscles in his back could keep his spine from snapping. Only the powerful muscles in his middle section could expand his diaphragm enough to allow oxygen into his lungs. "But... how... how, Father? How can you... heal me?"

Frederick Bethune lifted a pair of scissors from the pedestal nearest the anguished, inverted face of Tobias, as he answered. "You will glorify what God has given you... you will be reverent and thankful... and you will feel sensations never before known to you." He separated the two scissor blades, deftly slipping one between the loin covering and the inner thigh of his subject. "Never again will you want for anything, Tobias." He closed the blades together, cutting the fabric.

The mighty phallus was unleashed. Instantly, it sprang into the air, its momentum causing it to follow the belly of Tobias along its slight downward angle. There it lay in a state of normalcy. Even so, the length nearly reached his belly button, while its thickness matched the width of two fingers. Bethune was sure of it, because he laid two of his fingers along its shaft and gave a gentle rub.

"You will know pleasures unimaginable, Tobias." He removed his ceremonial robe, joining his subject in total nakedness. "You will sacrifice... you will rejoice... and you will never be tempted again. You will pass this test, my son, and I will help you."

Bethune circled to absorb this masculine beauty, ending his journey positioned between the spread-apart thighs of his prize. Directly below him at his waist level were two containers covered with soft skin and short, curly hairs. Stored inside was the seed of Tobias Corder. These two bulbous globes were not those of a man, but of a mighty steed. Frederick clenched his fist and lightly pressed it next to the skin. It measured three knuckles – it, not they. Each of this man's testicles, hanging comfortably from the base of his penis, isolated and vulnerable, measured three knuckles in diameter. Frederick Bethune nearly collapsed from the sight of them.

Regaining his composure, he bent at his waist, leaned down and laid his tongue onto the delicate skin, which caused Tobias to flinch in a useless attempt to defend himself.

"No, Father... please."

"Be strong, Tobias," Bethune mumbled between licks. "Have faith and I will give you heaven on earth."

Tobias was strong. He had no choice but to endure this assault upon him, as he struggled against his torturous position, valiantly gasping for air. Frederick tenderly kissed and caressed each orb one at a time, cradling with his tongue. His lavish praise was devoted to the left testicle until it was coated with spit, the youthful hairs darkened and pasted to the skin. He swiftly transferred his worship to the right gonad in the same manner, before returning to the left, never once breaking contact with his subject's globes or the skin separating them.

As he intensified his lathering, the eyes of Frederick Bethune witnessed the beginnings of surrender. It was the cock of Tobias Corder coming to life. Its thickness increased and its head began to traverse further along his belly. Bethune watched in amazement, as the powerful tool snaked past the navel, continuing its growth until a full one-third of the organ had pushed its way beyond the stretched hole in his belly. He removed his tongue from the testicles of Tobias and raised himself for a better view. The head of his subject's cock had slithered out from its protective covering, a tiny bead of syrup oozing from its mouth and dribbling onto the pit of his stomach. Frederick laid his open hand atop its lengthened shaft. Its width had expanded to three fingers.

With an intensified gusto, Frederick Bethune assaulted those heavenly balls, incorporating his lips into his method. He opened his jaw to capacity and encircled one of the orbs, massaging with lips above and below, licking with tongue everywhere else. After repeating this move on the other testicle, he launched a full-scale attack by rapidly peppering the nuts with kisses. He grasped tightening skin between his moistened lips and gently squeezed, then released to repeat the process again and again upon every inch of quickly-shrinking nuts.

Tobias was becoming desperate. "Please... Father... no more."

"Soon, Tobias." More tongue licks and lip squeezes were given.

Tobias began to groan between his pleadings, while still gasping for air. "How soon? Father, how long... must I... suffer?"

"Why do you suffer, Tobias? Do you not enjoy my touch?" Bethune brought his fingers into play, taking chunks of testicle skin between finger and thumb, then twisting them into corkscrews before releasing and repeating.
"My... my back... it is breaking in two... I... can't..."

"God has given you strength. Use it... use your glorious muscles."

"But... I can't... the pain..."

"What else, my son. What other pain do you feel?" His tongue worked on the nuts, maneuvering around and in between his fingertip corkscrews.

"Please, Father... don't... make me..."

"You must say it, Tobias, if you want my protection." His tongue licked in between his words. "Do not be afraid." He delicately scratched with his fingernails. "No words are forbidden here." His nails attacked the lower halves of the pitiful man's balls. "Where is your pain, Tobias?" He gingerly scratched and pinched, making circular paths from nuts to scrotum.

"Oh, God... have mercy." Tobias was nearly in tears. "My... my penis, Father. My penis... and my balls... they... they will explode... they... burn."

"Would you like me to ease your pain?"

"Yes... God, yes... please, Father."

"Will you sacrifice your seed to me?"

"Yes, Father... I will... I will give you... everything..."

Frederick Bethune took the engorged cock of Tobias Corder into his hand and lifted it vertical. He continued the motion until the tortured man's penis pointed directly towards him, perfectly horizontal, its pulsating shaft pressing down to compress his semen-bulging nuts. He took the gigantic, mushroom-shaped head into his mouth, wrapping his tongue beneath as though it were a blanket caressing the underside of a plump infant, then clamped the top side of his child with the roof of his mouth to seal in the warmth. He closed his lips. He encircled the thick, meaty shaft no more than one inch past the rim of its corona and sucked. Frederick sucked on the massive organ of Tobias in the same manner that a baby sucks on its mother's nipple, while lightly, but frantically, scratching with fingernails and fingertips the compressed, sensitive skin of majestic testicles.

Tobias Corder was ushered into a new world. As his body contorted and flexed to send one stream after another of his magnificent seed down to the gullet of Frederick Bethune, Tobias knew he would never again leave Egbert Castle. He would never have the desire to leave Egbert Castle, for the benefits of Bishop Bethune's protection could never be surpassed by anything or anyone. His verbal expressions proclaimed it; his orgasmic explosion confirmed it; and as Frederick completed the wholly-satisfying extraction of youthful bounty from his tortured gonads, Tobias begged for him to continue. Tobias surrendered himself to remain in his horrific, backward-arched position of bondage and allow Frederick to drain him again, with no interruptions, no time given for rest.

Bishop Bethune granted his request, but there was interruption. He unchained Tobias's feet and wrists, then lovingly lifted him with left arm supporting his back and right arm beneath the crook of his bent knees. Frederick carried the exhausted young man to his sleeping quarters and laid him on top of its soft mattress. Here, resting comfortably on his back, Tobias felt for the first time the warm confines of Frederick's innards. The rectal muscles of Frederick Bethune squeezed and prodded another burst of healthy seed from the all-consuming penis of Tobias Corder, as it flooded Frederick's bowels to further consecrate their union.

Heaven was promised to Tobias Corder. Heaven was delivered.

Part Nine – Secrets

"Look here, men, we have a visitor."

Peter Sion had Herman and Oscar take charge of Helena Sikes, then sent the escort guards back to their posts outside the Chamber of Inquisition.

"Those irons should do, and get rid of that sanctimonious dress. Bishop Bethune was not fooled, nor am I."

The two men violently yanked her clothing, ripping it to shreds and leaving her naked.

Sion picked up a strip of fabric. "Open her jaw." Herman clamped his powerful fingers onto the joint of her mouth and forced her teeth apart, at which time Sion wadded the fabric and stuffed it in between. After one more wadded ball of fabric filled her mouth, Helena was rendered speechless, her screams muffled. For sport, they let her believe she had escaped their grasp, and then all men stood laughing as Helena bolted for the door. Peter blocked her path, standing with arms folded.

"Eh wee ga!" She grabbed hold his shoulders and tried to push him aside.

"She struck me. Did you see that? Let you go, indeed." He casually pushed her towards the center of the room, where she stopped and looked all around for another route of escape. Finding none, the fear-stricken fool uselessly ran in all directions, her arms flailing and stuffed mouth babbling meaningless pleas for freedom.

"Like a chicken with no head," scoffed Otto.

"And that's when she's standing still," Herman added, as he violently grabbed her arm at her passing, nearly jerking it from her socket. "We've seen about enough."

With Oscar taking hold her other arm, they dragged Helena's feet along the stone floor in transporting the wretch to her bondage. Along the way, both of her shoes came off of her feet.

They locked her wrists into two irons attached to two chains that hung from the ceiling near the horizontal table. With shoes now removed, the balls of her bare feet were the only body parts touching the floor, while her arms were spread wide just above her head level. Two naked, vulnerable breasts presented a temptation to Sion, and he cruelly clutched his hands onto them, painfully crushing with clawed fingers.

"Well, my dear. Do you see what your lies have done?"

Helena's answer was to spit on her king. His response was to remove his hands from her tits, casually scrape with four fingers her saliva from his cheek and give the slime back to her, smearing it onto her breasts.

"Your true colors are revealed. Striking your king with your fists? Spitting in your king's face? Your chances of receiving mercy are dwindling by the second."

Peter Sion moved his face near to hers, daring Helena to spit on him again. She did not, but something caught his attention. He sniffed.

"What is that? Did you wear some sort of scent?"

Helena turned her head away, ashamed of her stupidity.

"You are nothing but a whore. Did you plan to seduce your Bishop as well? Or me?"

Peter moved away from her, the smell and sight of this woman turning his stomach. "It is doubtful you will ever feel guilt for any of this, but I will try to at least make you feel regret... for yourself, if for no one else."

With Sion walking away, Helena looked to her right. There was Jonathan, breathing heavily, his chin resting on his chest. Blindfolded, he could not see her, but he had recognized her voice. Jonathan had no desire to acknowledge her presence. He did desire to strangle her, but since he obviously was in no position to do so, he chose instead to ignore her altogether.

To Helena's left was William Corder, a mass of green goo covering his warm balls and erect penis. Tributaries of the congealing potion made creepy-finger lines along his downward-sloping belly. His eyes were closed. He was oblivious to the goings-on around him, because William was lost in an erotic dreamworld, a wanting desire to release the pent-up fluid of manly seed filling his testicles.

"Otto, another layer." Sion's order brought a ladle-full of fresh, stimulating goo and William's cock and balls received one more coating, while Peter moved behind his female prisoner.

"Now, my dear, watch." Prompted by Sion's pointing finger, Herman picked up his wooden pole.

"Mr. Sikes, prepare you belly," Peter kindly warned him.

Jonathan locked his abdominal muscles into a permanent hardness, not knowing when or where the spear would strike, and when it did, Herman's piercing pole was met by a solid wall of defense, a deep thud of wood penetrating muscle was coupled with a deep grunt of manly resistance. Herman drove his point home, impaling poor Jonathan midway between his navel and his pelvic bone.

"Ah, Wah, Gah!" Helena was heard to say with mouth forced agape. She tried to turn her head as the second pulverizing thrust was driven into the center of her husband's stomach, but Sion clutched a clump of her hair and yanked to his left, forcing her head to turn to the right.

"Herman, reverse your grip."

Sion's henchman unleashed a series of short, jabbing thrusts with his wooden spear from the pit of Jonathan's stomach to the lowest reaches of his belly.

It was necessary for Oscar to assist Peter Sion, because Helena Sikes had closed her eyes, refusing to witness the horror of Herman's assault upon her husband's tightened abdomen. On his own initiative, Oscar stood behind her left arm, placed the palms of his hands atop her head and dug his fingers into skin below her eyebrows, forcing open her eyelids with eight strong fingers.

"Look at that," Sion mocked her. "Listen to him groan. Look at those toes convulsing back and forth. And those beautiful muscles. Woman, are you insane? How could you deny a man such as this? He is glorious. Look at that massive chest. What is there not to love? What is there about him that could not satisfy you? Have you no heart? No soul? No brain?"

Sion allowed poor Jonathan to withstand this repeated jabbing assault for nearly one minute before calling upon Herman to withdraw his spear.

"It is shameful what you have done to him. Do you see his defiance? He holds his head strong, as though our tortures have no effect on him."

"Ghaw heh," she shrieked through her fabric-stuffed mouth. "Eh hiw ga."

"Stop it? Let him go? Woman, you must be insane. Look at that lower jaw jutting forward. Look at him thrust out that mighty chest. See those belly muscles? Why, it's almost as though he's inviting Herman to torture him some more. He's challenging us to grind that stake into him again. What an amazing man... heroic... majestic. Don't you wish you could go to him? Bury your face into him? Lick and kiss every inch of him? To think, you squandered such a golden opportunity. A man far superior to you. Far beyond what you deserve. You had him, but you cast him to the wolves. I am tempted to strangle you right here and now for your stupidity."

Helena said nothing – not because of her gagged mouth, but because Sion was correct. She was overwhelmed by his masculine strength. She did desire to run to him, to comfort him, to kiss and lick him, to smother his glorious form with her hands and her face. Sion was correct. Helena Sikes was filled with remorse – for her stupidity; for her opportunity lost; for her squandering of this gift.

Her chance to be the proper wife to this magnificent man had passed and it was her own doing. Helena's body started to collapse in defeat, but she was forced to swivel her head by Sion and Oscar, their hands working in unison.

"Look to your left, darling." Her bugged eyes were transfixed upon the form of William. "So, this is the man who raped you, is it?"

Helena made a feeble attempt to deceive once again by nodding her head up and down.

"Liar! Behold his mighty cock. It is a masterpiece of design and beauty. No woman would dare cry rape after feeling its power. Look at its length. Look at its breadth. It is perfection. It is not the penis of a man, but of a god. That is how I know you lied. His magnificent cock would silence the protests of any woman, whether it was forced upon her or not. You would never cry rape. You would cry 'More, William... More! Fuck me again and again and again!' That is exactly what you would say, you ignorant, cold-hearted witch."

Sion let go his grip on the woman's hair and Oscar released her head and eyelids, because she no longer fought them. Helena could not look away from William Corder's hypnotizing phallus, and Sion used it to further belittle her.

"No, this is your first encounter with William's mighty tool. Of this I am certain. Stimulating, isn't it, dear one? Mesmerizing. You never had his cock and you never will, because now, thanks to you, it belongs to me. For you, that glorious slab of man-meat represents another opportunity lost – another failure in your miserable life. Oh, you will see him perform, but William will perform for me – not for you."

Peter Sion's torture chamber came alive with activity. Oscar returned to his station, while Otto plastered on another layer of green potion. Herman was told to remove the blindfold from the eyes of Jonathan Sikes, while Peter Sion moved to the center of the room to supervise all.

"Helena Sikes, I want you to look your husband in the eye and confess. Tell him what you did. He will not believe what you say, but no matter. Tell him you are sorry. Tell him you are a fool for not loving him. Tell him that if you could reverse time and love him properly you would do exactly that. Say it with conviction. I might be able to convince Bishop Bethune that you should not be executed, depending upon your performance... depending upon your sincerity. Tell him."

Helena did tell him, in her garbled, mouth-stuffed ranting, as saliva dribbled down her chin and genuine tears streamed down her cheeks. Her body writhed and contorted in conjunction with her pleas, as she struggled with all of her strength to break free of the chains binding her. She yearned to approach her glorious, muscular husband, to drop on her knees before him and beg his forgiveness. And she tried to meet his eyes with hers, but was unable to do so.

This is because upon removal of his blindfold, Jonathan gave his wife not one glance. Instead, he focused his gaze upon his faithful friend, William. His eyes widened when he saw the green-coated penis extending over the top of William's belly button. His jaw dropped as he watched his companion writhing in unbridled ecstasy, arching his back and thrusting his chest into the air. He marveled in the fact that despite the confinement of William's elongated body to the rack, nothing could contain his wild acrobatics. Jonathan smiled at the sight of William curling his toes and the sounds of William groaning with lust, because William was happy. Right or wrong, William was feeling pleasurable sensations never before known. And because for Jonathan this was far preferable to watching William convulse and listening to William scream in agonizing pain, Jonathan was content. He did not understand how or why it was so, but William was not suffering. Now that he could see it – now that he could confirm it, Jonathan was bestowed with a sense of calm.

Peter Sion knew the reason for William's strained undulations – his majestic thrusting of chest into the air. William longed for something. It is a stimulation that for some men is merely an annoyance; but it is also a stimulation that for most men is everything, whether they have discovered it or not. Peter Sion took the ladle from Otto and filled it with goop. He sat on the step near William's head and slightly tilted the ladle, allowing a tiny stream to drop onto first his right nipple and then his left. The bound man's eyes opened and he recoiled from the searing heat, but Sion comforted him.

"Relax, William, do not worry. It will cool, just as before." He emptied the remaining potion onto William's penis and testicles, as the burning pain on his nipples subsided to a comforting warmth. His flinching resistance quickly transformed into the expansion of his chest and flattening of his belly. He posed and presented himself in the role of an all-powerful, manly hero. Feelings of masculine strength and dominance overwhelmed him. Massive doses of testosterone were released from testes to bloodstream, soon circulating and raging throughout. William lifted his head to admire his own chest, his own belly and his own cock and nuts. Upon seeing his magnificent organs, he thrust his hips into the air. He desperately made an attempt to trick his brain, to coerce his balls into releasing their bounty by means of a simulated fuck. But the friction necessary was not there. He clinched his scrotum, causing his glorious phallus to rise up off of his belly and present itself, suspended in mid-air. William's cock and his chest and his belly all rose into the air and begged to be worshiped, begged to be finished, and with no other way to express his lustful yearning, William cried out in anguish.

"Oh, god... Please, sire... Finish me. I cannot take this any more."

With a nod of his head, Sion signaled to Oscar, who grabbed the spoked wheel and slowly pushed upwards. William's body was stretched with a gradual and tormenting increase of tension, and as the ropes pulled his ankles bit by bit, the backside of his skin was scratched and splintered by the Steps to Purgatory. It was friction. Regardless that none of this friction was given to his cock or his nuts or his tits, it was friction nonetheless, and with an ear-shattering scream of orgasmic heaven, William's tortured cock spewed forth his manly seed. The initial volley peppered his chin. Subsequent spurts splattered his chest and stomach to mix white with green, transforming his skin into a glorious pallette of brilliance, a painting to represent the masculine power of man – the dominating, all-consuming masterpiece that is the male physique. It cannot be ignored and will not be denied.

Oscar allowed the tension to gradually lessen and gravity brought William down the steps. More back-side friction produced more spurts from his penis, as his weary testicles jettisoned one final round of semen from beneath their green shell.

"Peter, look." The voice came from across the room, where Herman was pointing to Jonathan Sikes. He was expanding himself, but it was not his muscles that were flexed. It was his bulge, his own penis trying to escape its loin covering. And as Peter Sion saw Jonathan's reaction, he moved to remove his prisoner's cock from its prison, grabbing the loin cloth and ripping it away.

A handsomely thick pole protruded directly forward, sturdy, just like its owner. Sion was awed by its strength and stood silently in admiration, but then felt wetness on the fabric. He dropped the cloth and raised his hand to see that his fingertips were covered with white goo – the spent seed of Jonathan Sikes.

Part Ten - The Savior

Men can hold their tongues. No matter what atrocities are perpetrated against them, if their very existence depends upon keeping what they know hidden, they will find a way to conceal what is known only to them.

But a man's penis does not lie. What Jonathan Sikes felt for William Corder could not be hidden. It majestically pierced the air for all to see. Its discharge oozed down the spread apart fingers of Peter Sion.

Jonathan shuddered at the sudden realization that he had been found out – that his secret was no longer his. But this fear was quickly replaced by anger, because to his left, Jonathan's wife was violently straining her body and jerking against her chains, while screaming indecipherable words at her husband.

"That's right, you ignorant whore," Jonathan sneered at her. "William and I have been carrying on for years – long before you were forced upon me. Kick and squirm all you like. Now, you know the truth. And I hope it sickens you... the same as you sicken me."

Helena was no longer kicking or squirming. Her body collapsed and she turned her head away in disgust, tears mixing with drool to coat her skin from cheeks to breasts.

"You are a fool, Helena. You could have shown me respect. You could have asked me to help you. Had you been honest... if you had ever shown one ounce of faith... of trust... in me... I would have solved your frustration. You could have had William any time you needed him. You could have had both of us at the same time... any time you desired."

Jonathan took several deep breaths of air, giving her a chance to answer, which she did not. All the while, Peter Sion stood silently and listened with interest while licking his fingers to taste Jonathan's manly seed. Peter also listened with joy in his heart, because Jonathan's words were doing more to destroy this woman than Peter ever could.

"William will do anything I ask of him," Jonathan continued. "How could you be so blind? Could you not feel the bonds between us?"

Helena answered no questions and nobody expected her to, especially Jonathan. "How does it feel, Helena?" How does it feel to know you could have had everything you wanted?"

Perhaps the thought had never occurred to Jonathan and perhaps it had, but his speech had brought him to the bitterest pill – the final dagger with which to once and for all rip Helena's heart to shreds.

"It is sad, Helena. And saddest of all, you could have had Tobias, too – had you done it the right way. That's right. William told me. What did you expect? Did you think he would keep such a thing from me?"

Peter Sion could not hold his tongue. An opportunity to thrust the knife in deeper had presented itself and he seized it.

"Oh, by the way, Jonathan. Your darling wife did have Tobias. She did feel his penis inside her, until my soldiers rescued him."

"No!" Jonathan cried out in anguish – then anger. "You evil bitch!" He violently tried to break free of his bondage. Every muscle flexed to capacity and his body twitched and jerked as though enveloped with electric eels. His outburst continued until he was exhausted, surrendered. Jonathan's body collapsed, his chin dropping to his chest, as he repeatedly mumbled to himself. "Oh, my god... oh, my god... oh... my... god."

Standing directly in front of the broken man, Peter tried to comfort him, knowing full well that he could not.

"Jonathan, she did not succeed. Helena felt him, but she did not receive him. Tobias is still pure. We arrived just in time."

He had no words for Peter Sion, and few remaining for Helena, but Jonathan did say them. They were the last words he would ever say to this treacherous woman. "We could have been very happy, Helena... the four of us, but thanks to you we will all die in this god-forsaken castle. You have destroyed us all... you foolish... heartless... bitch."

He turned his head away, resigned and defeated, but relieved that it was all over. Everything that should have been said had been said, and Helena Sikes had nothing to offer – no arguments, no begging forgiveness, only pathetic sobbing and moaning.

Oblivious to the entire scene and its speeches was William. For you see, Peter Sion's potion was a powerful thing. Never mind that William had jettisoned every drop of sperm his nuts could produce. Never mind that the potion itself was nearly dry. William's ecstatic stimulation and lustful writhing continued unabated. His genitals and nipples still yearned for the touch of anyone or anything. He laid with his eyes closed, hypnotized with a heightened sense of his own masculine power. His arching back thrust his chest and tits upwards. His clinching scrotum elevated his cock to hover in mid-air, seeking further stimulation.

Whereas at the end of his speech Jonathan was surrendered – no longer willing to fight his tormentors; no longer willing to imagine life beyond that dreadful torture chamber; no longer willing to dream of happiness with William or without – a glance to the writhing William renewed his defiance. The beauty of the man, both outer and inner, overwhelmed Jonathan. He was invigorated once more. All the joyous memories of his shared, secret life with William came to the forefront of his thoughts.

His dormant penis, made flaccid by the thought of Helena and his tirade against Helena, sprang to a newfound strength, proudly piercing the air in front of him. Jonathan would fight for the man he loved. If William was alive, so would he be, and he glared at Peter Sion with rage, expanding his chest and flexing his belly. "Do what you must, Sion. William and I will die like men."

Clearly, circumstances in the torture chamber had changed in a dramatic way. In fact, Peter Sion was so overcome by Jonathan's expression of devotion to his companion that he could not bear the thought of Frederick Bethune's continued absence. He made plans for leaving the torture chamber to seek the Bishop.

"Jonathan Sikes, you do not understand. No man will die here today... not you, not William."

Sion looked to his little bull. "Otto, I am proud of the work you and your men have performed today, and as your reward, you may take this woman to the table." He pointed to the round, horizontal table – Otto's table – directly behind her. "Strap her down and do with her as you please. I can only assume that there is something left of her vagina to keep you entertained. All I ask is that you keep her alive. Other than that, I could not care less."

Oscar, Herman and Otto wasted no time following the command of Peter Sion, while he gazed upon his handsome prisoner. "It is time for your release, Jonathan Sikes." He opened the leg irons. "You are free to do as you please." He positioned a ladder and climbed. "You may seek revenge on your wife." He raised one end of the bar above the hook upon which it had rested. "You may stimulate your friend, William." He lowered the bar below the hook. "But you will stay in this room for your entertainment, alongside Oscar, Herman and Otto."

Sion yanked the free end of the bar towards him, causing the other end to slide off of its hook. He let go the bar and Jonathan's feet hit the floor. At first, he was a bit unsteady, but as Sion stepped off the final rung of his ladder, Jonathan lunged towards him. He raised over his head the bar to which his wrists were still strapped and moved to strike Peter from behind, until he was violently jolted backwards, a massive arm wrapped around his neck. Within two seconds, Jonathan was spun around and his body slammed against the wall, and then before he could react to any of it, the metal bar was pressed firmly against his throat.

"You are a foolish man, Jonathan Sikes." Peter's little bull held Jonathan inches off the floor by means of that long bar pressing beneath his chin. "You are given your freedom. And this is how you repay your king? I should snap your neck right here and now."

Otto could easily have done just that. Regardless that Jonathan stood a full four inches taller than he; regardless that Jonathan was pressing the bar from his direction with all his might; the little bull was an unconquerable force, especially when the man he loved was being threatened.

"Thank you, Otto." Peter stood behind him. He kissed Otto's sweat-drenched hair, rested his chin upon Otto's bulging trapezoid, nibbled his over-sized ear, and rubbed with his hands up and down the length of Otto's flexing, sweat-slicked, fur-matted chest and belly. "You amazing, strong-ass, son of a bitch." He smothered Otto's thick, smooth-shaven neck with kisses. He tugged the hair on the nape of that neck with his lips. "God, I love you... you fucking he-man... my savior... coming to my rescue again."

Sion turned his attention to Otto's prisoner. "You do not understand, Jonathan. My little bull could kill you in an instant, if I give the word." Peter clamped fingers and thumbs onto his little bull's perfectly round, tiny and sharp-tipped nipples. "Do you see the steam... coming from his nostrils? He waits for my command." Peter twisted those nipples, causing his little bull to snort, mucus landing onto Jonathan's stomach.

Jonathan's face was red, quickly turning purple. "Relax on him, Otto.

I will explain to Jonathan his good fortune."

Otto eased his pressure, but kept the bar firmly in place, as Jonathan sucked in oxygen with all his strength.

"You are here for my enjoyment, nothing more. Tell me truth... was your pain really so great?"

Jonathan turned his head no – with difficulty.

"Do you not realize that Herman could have run you through, had that been my intent?" Peter released his little bull's tits and resumed hand-rubbing his chest and belly. "Think, Jonathan. You were brought here for my entertainment. Your stupid wife made that possible. Little did I know that you and William were one. Now that I do, you and William are one with us. You can join us and enjoy pleasures never before known to you; or you can continue to fight us. Choose number two and by the powers of hell I *will* do you in. This is your final chance. Do you join us?"

Jonathan eagerly nodded yes.

With a final tweaking of his little bull's nipples, Peter spoke to his compact package of muscle. "It is good, Otto. Between the woman and William, I think you four men will have plenty to keep you occupied until my return."

Before exiting, Peter turned for one final glance. Herman and Otto were busy with the roping of Helena Sikes to the table; Otto was unstrapping the bar from Jonathan's wrists; William continued to writhe in unbridled ecstasy. Peter Sion hated to leave this room, but he knew Frederick would never forgive him if he did not invite his friend to participate. The recent revelations in the torture chamber were unprecedented. Peter could only imagine what dramas were yet to play out.

Part Eleven - The Powers That Be

Sion could barely contain his excitement, but as he traversed the corridor and stairwell leading out of the dungeon he reflected upon how, once again, Otto had come to his rescue. This led him to recall what up until then had been his most harrowing experience in the torture chamber. These were memories suppressed, for it was an event in which the sanity of Peter Sion was nearly lost to this world. With no warning, triggered by the events of today, these thoughts now bubbled forth from the depths of his mind, causing him to stop where he stood.

Six years prior there were three men brought to the dungeon, and unlike Jonathan Sikes and William Corder, these men were there for very serious reasons. They were charged with thievery and murder, crimes for which they received treatment unparalleled in the history of Sion's torture chamber.

The Gavin Gang had terrorized the roads leading into Grunewald for many months. Of course, no one spoke of Thomas Gavin and his gang of three by this name until they were captured. Before that they were known simply as "The Bandits." They struck with cunning, emerging on horseback from the dark cover of thick forest growth. They targeted the weak, hapless and unarmed farmers returning from auction in nearby settlements.

With one draft horse pulling an empty wagon that had delivered his goods, the slow-moving farmer would be easy prey for Gavin and his men, as they sneaked from behind to halt their victim's wagon. They threatened him with swords and daggers, forced him to give up whatever pittance he had received from the sale of his goods, and then allowed him to continue safely home.

To Peter Sion, they were a thorn. Despite the best efforts of his best soldiers, Sion could not capture Thomas Gavin and his men, and this became a threat to his reputation. After all, what would other men of power think of him, once word got out that he could not even apprehend a petty gang of thieves?

He took matters into his own hands, launched his own expedition and was nearly killed in the process. The story is well-known.

During his recovery, Sion issued a decree (actually, it was Otto's decree in the name of Peter Sion) that no villagers were to venture from his manse without an armed escort of Sion soldiers, and for many weeks this quelled the rash of robberies. The Bandits seemed to have either changed occupations or made the decision to terrorize elsewhere – or at least that is what everyone had assumed. For the time being, calm was restored to Grunewald.

George Corder was proud of his draft horses. His were known as the strongest and most agreeable in temperament of any to be found within Sion's realm. He would on occasion receive requests for the seed of his stallions – a stud service – for which he was paid a worthwhile fee. Overly-protective, he did not allow mares to mix with those of his stable, and therefore would escort the stallion himself to breed with his client's mare on his client's property. His wife Marian accompanied him on these journeys, which sometimes required overnight stays in waiting for the mare to accept the copulation and for the stallion to plant his seed.

George Corder also was a pig-headed man. He had no love for Peter Sion and no intention of requesting anything from that "tyrant," as he called him, nor would he accept the advice or offer of his good friend Sebastian Sikes.

"You must not go this alone. If you won't ask for armed escort, at least allow me to go with you and Marian. Perhaps if they see two men, these bandits will look for easier prey."

Corder gallantly scoffed at the suggestion. "Those thieves are nowhere near. They have not been heard from or seen for weeks. I have traveled this road many times. I know every tree and every stone. If anything is amiss, I will instantly recognize it and bolt for safety."

Sebastian knew the man was not to be convinced and abandoned the argument, but he did make one final request.

"Please, at least take this with you." He handed George Corder his long-blade knife, kept in his own house for the protection of his own family.

"For you, I will take it with me."

"To hell with me. Take it for yourself and your wife."

Leaving his two boys William and Tobias in the care of Sebastian Sikes, George Corder loaded his stallion into his self-made, low-floored wagon, hitched it to his best, duo team of sturdy draft horses and began their journey. He and his wife would never again see their village of Grunewald.

It was one thing to be petty thieves – an annoyance and a threat, to be sure, but thanks to George Corder, the Thomas Gavin gang elevated themselves to the status of killers. Not only did Corder slash the face of one bandit, he also managed to puncture the gut of another and leave a deep gash in the arm of Gavin himself. Such was the effectiveness of the knife given to him by Sebastian Sikes, but in the end it could not save George Corder or his wife. Because their masks of concealment had fallen in the melee, Marian Corder had seen their faces. Three of the bandits were unknowns, but one face was instantly recognized. It was the face of Thomas Gavin, who had been raised from birth in the village of Grunewald. For this, Marian Corder joined the corpse of her husband to lie on the ground, dragged beneath their wagon for make-shift concealment by those who murdered them both.

It was blood that did them in, that and loyalty to one another. Refusing to leave any companion behind whether injured mortally or superficially, Gavin's gang traveled slowly, leaving easily-tracked drops of blood with every step. Sion's soldiers found the corpse of a man with stains on his clothing of dark red from sternum to knee within 48 hours. The remaining three, including Thomas Gavin, were captured 12 hours later.

They did not take their quarry through the village of Grunewald, but to a back entrance of Egbert Castle. Had the villagers seen the prisoners, they would have torn each man to pieces from limb to limb. Such was the sorrow felt for the loss of George and Marian Corder. The tragedy of two orphaned boys only intensified the grief consuming Grunewald – and the anger.

Bishop Bethune and Peter Sion did not bother with the Chamber of Inquisition. These men were taken directly to the cleanup cell and then to the torture chamber. While Frederick did the paperwork, Sion did the unpleasantries.

The instruments of torture were put to their true purpose on this day. The man on the horizontal table was mercilessly stretched in four directions. He was sliced and carved with bullwhips and floggers, until his entire body resembled the bloody gash left on his face by George Corder. The man on the Board of Impalement felt the full force of Herman's strong arms – not a pole as endured by Jonathan Sikes, but a wooden club, which Herman swung from the side with merciless velocity. And the man's belly was not the half of it. Sion gave Herman free reign to strike his victim wherever he chose to do so, producing the popping and cracking sounds that accompany the breaking of ribs of the chest and bones of the legs and arms. The loin covering was not necessary, because Herman was allowed to crack the pelvis as well. And besides, nobody was concerned with the amount of feces and urine and blood that came from the man's insides.

Sion reserved the Steps to Purgatory for Thomas Gavin. It was the only proper choice for the man who had instigated so much grief for Peter and everyone else in his realm. Oscar's strength exerted triple the pressure of that applied to William Corder, permanently separating joints and tendons, while Otto climbed the steps wearing the boots of his soldiering days to stomp on Thomas Gavin's racked body from his shins to his chest.

Already in a weakened state from loss of blood and days on the run, all three men quickly confessed to every robbery but one. None of them would confess to either the robbery or murder of George and Marian Corder, and for this they received the wrath of Peter Sion. For this, they were introduced to a Peter Sion that even he himself did not know.

He brewed a potion in his kettle – not the stimulating kind, but a mixture of evil and desecration. It's color was red, not green. When poured onto skin, the potion's initial searing did not subside, but grew worse. Its acidic qualities caused the flesh to bubble. The intensifying, chemically-charged heat caused the skin to melt and to rise with hideous blisters and boils, and the pain accompanying this foul potion was more than any man could bear.

One by one, each man felt the agony of Sion's liquid from hell, starting with the man on the table. Sion's ladle was emptied onto the man's feet, and then Sion traversed the wretched soul's body with layers upon his shins and thighs, until he heard the words required. He began to order the bringing of water-filled buckets to wash away his horrific mixture, but inexplicably stopped himself in mid-sentence. Peter Sion was not satisfied that the man had admitted his foul deed, preferring instead to hear the tortured screams coming from the table for no good reason – other than his insatiable appetite for revenge. He left that man to suffer, while moving to his next victim.

For this man, the man on the Board of Impalement, Sion reversed his approach. He splattered the contents of his ladle onto the man's chest, then watched with glee as the burning potion ran trails of destruction down the front side of his torso. The evil fingers congealed, extending to the lowest reaches of the man's belly. With howls of agony to his right and directly in front of him, Sion targeted another assault of burning liquid directly to the man's genitalia. The agonizing potion traveled down both thighs and shins, even reaching so far as to sear the skin between his toes. And again, the words of confession did not end the man's shrieking agony, as Peter Sion's cruelty usurped rational thinking. He allowed the liquid to remain, turning the man's flesh into boiling goo.

If Oscar, Herman and Otto had thought Peter Sion was consumed with an unprecedented zeal for depravity, they had yet to see the worst. For you see, Thomas Gavin would defy him to the very end. No amount of horrific liquids could loosen his tongue, and as one layer after another failed to produce the results he desired, Peter Sion became enraged beyond the limits of a sane man. He repeatedly ran to his kettle for one dose after another, his ears deaf to the pleas of his henchmen as they shouted words of reason to him. Even Otto, his closest and most trusted assistant, could not break through Peter's barrier of madness, and in fear for his own sanity, fearful of losing the man he loved, Peter's little bull took matters into his own hands.

Otto dispatched Oscar to fetch Bishop Bethune, and then he and Herman used their buckets of water to wash away the agony of the other two men. Oblivious to this was Peter Sion, who dribbled yet another ladle-full of evil onto the wholly-encased body of Thomas Gavin. The pitiful man contorted and writhed beneath layers of searing entombment, which included his genitals and his face and his head. The horrific sounds coming from his mummified form were not of this world, but of the underworld – from the grave.

It had to be done. For the first time ever, Otto defied his king. He and Herman grabbed hold of Peter Sion. They subdued him, locked his wrist into one of the hanging chains, and then they frantically dumped one bucket after another of rinsing water onto Gavin's tortured skin.

What greeted them, and what greeted Frederick Bethune when he entered with Oscar closely behind him, was a sight of grotesque destruction. It was a scene dragged from the depths of hell; a melding of white, red, black and purple; a carnage of seared and still bubbling flesh melted to exposed muscle, vein and bone; a mass of horrific meat with no eyes, no hair, no ears, no genitals, no fingers, no toes and no lips. It was nothing more than a hulk on a descending staircase, dotted by 10 black nails and two breathing holes. The holes gurgled and hissed.

It was breathing.

No carnage of battle, no witness to severed limbs, crushed skulls or punctured organs could have prepared the three soldiers for what they saw. All three regurgitated where they stood.

Frederick Bethune turned away from the nightmare, focusing his eyes and ears onto the ranting of a madman.

"Look, look at that." Peter Sion pointed to the steps with his free hand, his eyes wild and red, his mouth frothed with spit. "See what happens? Defy me, will you? Attack me, will you? He'll talk... you ask him... oh, yes... he will talk... no man escapes me... thought you could kill me, did you? Oh, no... you'll talk... you will pay... ask him... talk, damn you... go ahead... ask him."

Bethune closed his eyes in meditation. He closed his mind to the cackling of Peter Sion and opened it to communication from elsewhere, from a source in which he believed. And if a man believes strongly enough in his source, if his conviction supercedes all earthly thought and belief, then the answers will come to him. Whether the answers come from another place and time or whether they come from the depths of a man's brain and were there all along is irrelevant – Frederick Bethune sought solution for his friend and found it.

Peter Sion was taken to the chapel devoted to the Bishop of Grunewald. There, he was placed to sit on the alter. Oscar, Herman and Otto roped his ankles, roped his wrists, roped his arms to his torso and laid him upon his back in a bound bundle. They locked the door when exiting the chapel, leaving behind the Bishop and his subject.

For nearly six hours Frederick Bethune ministered to him. He told the still-babbling Peter Sion about what is known in the Christian faith as "The Father," of how and why it is the beginning of the Lord's Prayer, supposedly composed by Jesus Christ himself. He told the meaning of its opening phrase, "Our Father," and that these two words are the only words necessary to define the faith. Our Father encompasses all, and therefore, we are all brothers and sisters, all from one seed and all equal.

As the mumbling ceased and Peter Sion's lips fell silent, Frederick told of the glory of man, of how the spirit inside can be good or bad and can be changed from bad to good. Either way, the spirit inside is equaled in beauty by the vessel that contains it. The body of man is to be worshiped. It is to be placed on an alter and praised. It is a work of art – a masterpiece of design and engineering, powered by the perfect combination of muscle, joints, tendons and bone. It is a gift from God and a representation of God. Therefore, the body of man is to be cherished as a god.

One could claim that the salvation of Peter Sion was a miracle; one could also claim that he simply was weary of listening to Bethune's spiritual mumbo-jumbo and schemed for his release, but the end result is that Peter Sion walked through those chapel doors exorcized of his madness.

And although he never fully accepted the Christian faith in its entirety, he did accept the core. He did fancy the idea of spiritual Father and sons, with sons as brothers. He did enthusiastically cling to the worship of man, or more precisely, men. It is the one thing coming from his session with Bishop Frederick Bethune that could be claimed without question. Peter Sion had found his inner voice. He listened to that voice and put the glory of the male physique on the pedestal to which it belonged, reserving the highest alter, or course, for his beloved Otto.

To appease the villagers of Grunewald, two still-alive killers were given to them and they proceeded to disassemble the bodies until lifeless. The nightmare of what once was Thomas Gavin died upon the Steps to Purgatory during Peter Sion's session of mental healing, but as atonement for his sins, Peter Sion altered the truth of Thomas Gavin. His became a story of legend. It was Gavin's Gang, no doubt, but no murderer was he. Gavin had actually tried to prevent the killing of George and Marian Corder, but the numbers were against him. Stricken with remorse over what his companions had done, Gavin sought the soldiers of Peter Sion and led them to their quarry, but sadly, he had received such grave injury in defense of the Corders that Thomas Gavin died in the arms of Peter Sion himself. Gavin received a proper burial, concealed in closed casket and laid to rest on the grounds of Grunewald Cathedral, where he was to receive the reverence and respect of all who visited him.

This version of the story was Peter Sion's first act as a changed man. It was done to preserve the family's name and it was done with charity, for rather than scorn, the parents of Thomas Gavin received pity and praise. Their son lived as a thief, but died as a hero.

Tank Books

Part Twelve - Dreams

Bethune was not at all pleased when he heard the pounding on his chamber door.

"Frederick, I must speak with you. It is of utmost importance."

Recognizing the voice of Peter Sion, Bethune responded with civility, but also with agitation. "I am resting. What is it?"

"It is our prisoners. I need your assistance immediately."
"Very well. Give me one minute."

He stood up to retrieve his sleep robe, then started for the door, but was interrupted by a whispering Tobias. "No, Frederick. Please, don't let him in here."

Bishop Bethune returned to the bed where Tobias lay naked underneath the coverings. "Do not worry. There are no judgments here."

"No, Frederick. It is too soon. Meet him at the door."

He compassionately kissed the young man's forehead and relented. "I understand. He will not enter here."

Frederick and Tobias had come far in the few short hours they had been together. Once in the Bishop's bed, the experience of forced orgasm while chained had transformed into one of unbridled, mutual admiration. It certainly was no accident that these two men had grown so close so quickly. Both had been groomed for this encounter for many years, although only one had planned, hoped and dreamt of it becoming reality.

Tobias Corder had first come to the attention of Frederick Bethune upon the death of the young man's parents, courtesy of Thomas Gavin and his gang of three.

It was required of Sebastian Sikes to seek the blessing of Bishop Bethune in order to permanently take the Corder boys into his home. Sebastian had been the closest friend to George Corder and his family, plus his own sixteen-year-old son Jonathan was exactly the same age as William and both had grown up nearly as brothers. The presence of these five – Sebastian, Martha and Jonathan Sikes; William and Tobias Corder – in the official court of Peter Sion was the beginning of Frederick's unexplainable interest in young Tobias. His unruly, sand-colored hair, sturdy bones and rapidly-developing, stable-boy musculature caught the Bishop's attention immediately, but something deeper struck Frederick Bethune.

It was the eyes of Tobias. There was a near-to-spiritual connection, made stronger by the youth's brave posture. He stood tall and proud for a twelve-year-old, seeming to be unshaken by the tragedy that had befallen him. The dazzling and intimidating ceremonial garb worn by Bishop Bethune did not faze him in the least, and when the young man looked into his Bishop's eyes, a connection was made. Frederick sensed that this boy was god-sent to him for good purpose and he knew that they were destined to meet again.

He would monitor Tobias Corder very closely through his spies, year after year, always aware of every important event in the life of Tobias, as he grew in stature from that of a boy to that of a strong, virile man. And just as the death of the elder Corders had brought them their first meeting, the treachery of Helena Sikes had brought Frederick Bethune and Tobias Corder to their final meeting – their forever together meeting.

It was William Corder who unknowingly prepared Tobias for his

Bishop. William's motherly, over-protective doting upon his younger brother prevented Tobias from discovering the sensual joys of his body. He kept very tight reins upon which persons of the female gender could speak to or interact with Tobias, lest some form of exploratory fondling progress to an accidental corruption. He even convinced young Tobias that touching himself was an abomination to God, and that since God sees all, he had best keep his hands off. This myth was effective despite the fact that William and Jonathan carried on nightly, mutual masturbation sessions upon their shared bed in the very same room where Tobias slept. So deeply ingrained were these repressions that even at the age of eighteen years, Tobias gave no thoughts to dousing the raging fire in his loins. He repeatedly convinced himself that only with marriage could he release this pressure, and no temptations by any female could stir him from his conviction – until the appearance of Helena Sikes. So lustful she, so persistent she, that Tobias was broken of his self-imposed shell, hypnotized and mesmerized by an erection that could not be denied.

Frederick Bethune snatched his prize from the temptress just in the nick of time. For Tobias, the first-ever release of his pent-up sperm came from atop the pedestal of a marbled column, coerced by the wet, warm, tantalizing lips and tongue of a hungry mouth – a man's mouth – the mouth of Frederick Bethune. For six long years Frederick had waited to worship this beautiful phallus, and once he had opened the floodgates, there was no stemming the flow.

"Father..."

"Shhhh," Frederick quieted his young steed while gently gliding up and down his mighty pole. "You must call me Frederick. Do not talk. Close your eyes and dream – dream of any pleasure you desire."

"But why, Fath... Frederick?" Tobias lay on his back with arms sprawled. He was in the same position on the same mattress to where his Bishop had transported him following their journey from chapel to bedroom. "Why did you torture me?"

"I torture you still, Tobias. Mine is the torture of delights." Bethune sat with buttocks pressing onto the young man's pelvis, crushing the entire length of his mighty tool with the needing muscles inside his rectum. "It was necessary to chain you. Otherwise, you would have resisted me and never known what was to come. I made you feel. It was necessary for you to feel both pain and pleasure, Tobias, so that your mind would not interfere. And now you know."

"What? What do I know?"

"Trust, Tobias." He raised his buttocks, inches at a time until the rim of his ass held only the corona of the penis. "I could have punished you in any manner I desired... the whip... pinchers... my fists." He began his return journey down the long shaft, crushing its width with every inch of descent. "But I did not punish you, because I care for you, Tobias. I chose to worship you, just as I worship you now. Close you eyes and dream, Tobias. Let us speak with no more words."

Tobias did close his eyes and spoke no more. He dreamed of nothing, for he knew not what to dream. Instead, he focused on the incredible sensations caressing his penis – the powerful, squeezing, undulating vise, its warm friction eliciting an explosive, second-time orgasm, which for Tobias was more fulfilling than the first. It is the knowing of what will come that gratifies. The knowing of a second-coming heaven supercedes the unknowing, virgin surprise.

Exhausted, Tobias rolled onto his side. Sleep was a welcomed respite for him.

For Frederick, sleep would not come. He patiently waited during the next hour, laying behind his youthful prize and admiring the broad, muscular back and shoulders while gently massaging them with fingertips. Soon, Tobias was able to dream undisturbed. He dreamt of being made to roll onto his back. He dreamt of wetness scraping the thick soles of his feet and tender skin between his toes. He dreamt of lips kissing his shins and calves, of lips gently tugging the hairs of both. He dreamt of a nose and lips and an entire face pressing onto his belly, with an occasional tongue painting the rim of his navel. In his dream, there were kisses planted onto his pectorals and thumbs gently scraping the tips of his nipples. There were lips kissing his nipples and lips pinching them, which came between words that were praising him. In his dream, there were many words from one voice – words of devotion and of promises. The words came in flurries, between kisses and licks and loving pinches, and they spoke of wonders unimaginable to him – of visits to cities unknown; of foods never before tasted and drinks never before swallowed; of fabrics and jewels never before worn. And then, there were no more words, only praise. Oral praise was lavished onto his testicles and penis. Manual praise was lavished onto his chest, his nipples, his belly. And as his dream ended, he awoke to the convulsions of an orgasmic explosion unlike any that he could dare to dream. And there was Frederick, accepting the erotic dream of Tobias into his mouth, into his gut, ingesting the seed into his very being.

With his dream transformed to reality, all apprehensions for Tobias were swept away. Frederick Bethune was no longer his Bishop, but his protector, his mentor, his life force. The energy of youth swept over him – a wave of senses – of gratitude, security, respect and admiration. Charged with this energy, Tobias rose to grasp the shoulders of Frederick, maneuvering him to lie on his back where Tobias had just been. His lips and tongue worshiped the older man, same as the older man had worshiped him, until this unchecked, youthful energy caused him to take Frederick's knees into his grasp. He lifted Frederick's legs and draped them over his own shoulders. Tobias overwhelmed Frederick Bethune with his dominating enthusiasm for what was new, what was indescribably pleasurable, masculine and right. He infused the older man with his youthful energy, and in the process, allayed all lingering fears that it could ever end.

"I will never leave you, Frederick. You will have to chase me away."

Tank Books

Part Thirteen – The Smell of Man

With Tobias safely hidden as a covered lump in his bed, Frederick cracked open the door to address his friend.

"What is it, Peter."

"We were wrong about these men. Jonathan and William are much more clever than we could have imagined."

"Give me five minutes. I will meet you in the Grand Hall."

As the footsteps of Peter Sion faded, Frederick peeled away the covers and lavished the chest of Tobias with kisses. "Wait here. I will send you food and drink."

"Where are you going?" Tobias was more than ready to entertain his lover with another round of passion.

"There is business which requires my attention. I won't be long."

"Should I dress?"

The kisses stopped and Frederick scanned the glorious physique laying before him. "Tobias, you never need dress again, if that is your wish."

Frederick Bethune quickly made himself presentable and left Tobias, locking the door behind him. He descended the staircase and there was Peter Sion pacing the floor with hands behind his back.

"Peter, what has happened?"

"Frederick, we were terribly mistaken about these two men."

"How so?"

"Since the day the Corders joined the Sikes family, Jonathan and William have been one."

"Impossible."

"No, it is true. Jonathan has confessed it."

"How did this escape us? Our spies would surely have seen. How could they have kept this hidden from us all these years?"

"I do not know. As I said, they are much more clever than we could have imagined."

"Then you must release them. Can you control them?"

"William is still transfixed by my potion. Jonathan is cavorting with Otto and his men but still under their control. That is, assuming he took my advice to join them. If not, Otto has probably killed him."

"Very well. Take them to a cell and care for them. I will join you after my dinner."

Bishop Bethune lied about that. He had meals prepared and took them himself on a tray to his room where Tobias waited, still naked and very, very hungry. As for Sion, he no longer was concerned with Frederick's lack of participation in the torture chamber. All he really sought from the Bishop was an official "church" blessing to release his prisoners from their bondage, since they were brought to Egbert Castle charged with "church" crimes.

Helena Sikes was well cared for during Sion's absence. Her entertainment was ongoing when he returned. He found the configuration rather fascinating, as Herman lay atop the spread-eagled woman with his penis in her vagina. Apparently, Otto and Oscar had already planted their seeds into her, because Helena offered no resistance. The all-consuming power of these men had effectively subdued her to the point that even her mouth was cooperating. Otto, with legs spread outside her shoulders, had replaced her cloth stuffing with his cock stuffing. He laid with his belly pressing her nose and was gallantly fucking the back of her skull. This left plenty of room for Herman to nestle his head near Otto's butt crack and voraciously devour her tits with his mouth. Beyond Otto was Oscar, his legs draped over her spread and chained arms. He sat with his butt near the edge of the table, his cock in Otto's mouth to complete the configuration.

Sion stood quietly near the doorway, refusing to disturb the scene before him. To his right, William continued to writhe with unfulfilled want, the green potion now dark and congealed on his penis, testicles, belly and chest. To William's left, Jonathan was contentedly sitting on the step near William's chest with a smile on his face, gleefully watching as three dominant males ravaged a helpless female.

Peter took a deep breath. He took several deep breaths. The room was rank with masculinity – the smell of sweat, of ass sweat, of cock and ball sweat, of arm pit sweat and foot sweat. Sion absorbed all of it with his nose and his eyes and his ears, until he began to sweat. His was the sweat of excitement – an uncontrollable urge to remove every ounce of briny sweat from every man in that room.

"Jonathan, why are you not helping them? Give your wife one final thrill."

"I have no wife. Besides, there's no room."

Peter joined him on the steps, taking a seat on the other side of William's chest. "Then why are you not taking care of William?"

"I was waiting for you."

"That is a lie. You have lived in fear for too long."

While William moaned and writhed in his erotic dreamland, Sion and Sikes watched the three men on the table.

"Did you speak to William?" Sion asked.

"Yes."

"Did he tell you of the potion?"

"Yes, but he was not speaking to me, only to himself."

Peter took a deep breath, as he watched the three work on the woman. "Ah, can you smell that?"

"Smell what?"

"The smell of men. Men at work... men at play."

Jonathan inhaled deeply. "Sour... burns my nose."

Peter smiled. Obviously, the aromas of the torture chamber did not invigorate Jonathan. In contrast, Peter could hardly contain himself. And with no men in the room, bound or otherwise, who could care less, Peter suddenly realized that there was no reason for him to contain himself.

"You know, Jonathan, I have also lived a part of my life in secret."

"How so?"

"Those men, right there on the table. You see, the bedroom is for love, but this torture chamber is for men. For twenty-two years I have seen these men exert amazing energy... watched them work... seen them sweat. And not once have I ever taken advantage of the masculinity in this room... not with them."

"They are more like beasts, not men."

It was not a kind statement, but Peter understood that his was not a common desire. Peter was thrilled to have manly beasts and their odors available to him. He vowed to himself right then and there that he would not squander one more minute of the twenty-two-years-worth that had already passed.

"I have no more secrets, Jonathan... nor should you."

He descended the steps, leapt onto the table and untangled Otto, Oscar and Herman. He laid them out one by one on top of her, Herman across her shins, Otto across her middle and Oscar across her breasts. With their backsides laying perpendicular atop the bound female and their arms sprawled beyond their heads, Peter Sion began his assault.

Beginning at the woman's foot end, he buried his face into Herman's belly. He extended his tongue to taste the salt, breathing deep to smell the brine. He licked away layers of sweat from belly to chest. He licked the rank arm pits, burning his nose with their manly aromas. He lavished Herman's forehead, nose and cheeks with kisses, scraping his face against the one-day's stubble. And with a shift to his left, he started working on Otto where he had finished working on Herman, assaulting him from his face to his belly. Another shift brought him to Oscar and his journey took him from his belly to the sweat-matted hair, his nose pressing the scalp of Oscar's head.

Peter Sion licked and swallowed each man's sweat until their skin was dry, and then returned to Herman, where he slavishly worshiped his nuts. He tasted sweat of a different flavor; he inhaled the nearby fumes of hairy ass. He slavishly buried the penis to the back of his throat and finished what the vagina had not. Herman was licked clean and drained dry, as was Otto, as was Oscar.

One, two, three, Sion's loyal assistants were relieved of their masculine juices, inside and out.

"Men, let us join Jonathan Sikes on the Steps to Heaven. We all must tend to poor William."

Three hulking male physiques removed themselves from the crushed form of a gasping-for-air female. She was abandoned on her table of torment, while the three stepped down from the table and followed Peter.

"Come, Jonathan," Sion invited. "It is time for William to finish."

Peter filled the ladle and applied a fresh coat of goo to William's cock and balls, while Oscar, Herman and Otto climbed past Jonathan to position themselves along the length of William's undulating form. His painting finished, Peter Sion sat on the same step as Jonathan with William's inverted face between them.

Jonathan cradled his companion with both hands. He lifted William's head and called his name. His eyes opened. William grinned with pleasure. "Oh, god, Jonathan. It is like nothing I've ever known. There are no words to describe for you what I feel right now."

Their lips came together, while eight more lips laid themselves onto William's skin. Jonathan's tongue probed the back of William's throat. William's tongue responded to taste the inside of Jonathan's cheeks.

Countless kisses, licks and gentle pinches came from eight masculine lips, as all-consuming rubs and squeezes came from eight masculine hands. And although nothing was there to love his penis and testicles except for the stimulating goo, these things were enough. Eight hands, eight pairs of lips, Sion's potion and Jonathan's kiss triggered William's cock. Its initial volley jettisoned into the hair of his beloved Jonathan. Subsequent spurts sent unfathomable streams of white semen to once again paint his belly and chest.

From the horizontal table, Helena Sikes raised her head to peer over her breasts. She helplessly watched, ostracized by the men she once had, but did not want. Never again would she know the love of any man.

"Jonathan, please... do something"

They looked at her, smiled and turned away.

With another layer plastered, Jonathan locked lips with the man he loved, and the five-man worship of William Corder began anew.

Tank Books

Part Fourteen - Sleep Well, Men

"What will you tell my brother?"

Tobias asked the question between succulent chunks of roasted pig, delivered to his mouth by the fingers of Frederick.

"In the morning, you can tell him yourself."

"Will you go with me to his house?"

"He is here. I will take you to him."

"Here?" Tobias was startled by this news, swallowing whole the not-yet-chewed morsel of pork in his mouth. "What is he doing here?"

How could he have known? Frederick had seen to it that Tobias knew nothing of his brother's fate, nor that of Jonathan and Helena Sikes.

The Corder brothers had not shared the same home since two years after the death of their parents, William having left the Sikes's household in his eighteenth year, taking residence in the house his father had built and resurrecting the family name in the business of draft horses. At the suggestion of Bishop Bethune, Sebastian and Martha Sikes kept Tobias in their household as he matured from adolescence to manhood. At age seventeen he obtained his apprenticeship at the blacksmith shop. At two weeks past his eighteenth birthday Helena Sikes made her play for him. He was stricken with fear for his own well-being when the soldiers of Peter Sion dragged him from her bed, and now Tobias felt that same fear for his brother.

"What has William done? Who brought him here?"

"I brought him here to answer false accusations made against him."

"What accusations? Who made them?"

"Helena Sikes."

With jaw dropped in stunned realization, Tobias quietly listened to the sordid tale of Helena's folly, and of how he, William and Jonathan were caught in her web of deceit. Of course, Frederick failed to mention the activity in Sion's torture chamber, choosing instead to bring Tobias up to date with the current situation.

"Do not worry. The woman is locked away in a holding cell. Peter and I knew of her trickery from the beginning. Your brother and Jonathan are in the care of Peter Sion. He is entertaining them as we speak."

The reputation of Peter Sion was such that Tobias still was uneasy. "Are the rumors of him true?"

"What rumors are those, Tobias?"

"That he tortures people."

"Yes, it is true, but only people who incur his wrath. Only people who have broken the law. To those, he is a terror. To good men, he is just."

"And you?"

"I uphold the laws of the church. It is the same as with Peter. William and Jonathan are good men. They are guilty of nothing and are in good standing with Peter. During their stay here, they have become friends to him."

"Peter Sion is also your friend?"

"Yes, he is." Frederick placed his hand to the shoulder of Tobias and pulled him close, until their faces were inches apart and eye to eye. "Tobias, can you not see? You know the people of Grunewald. Some of them might take matters into their own hands. We cannot have some woman making false accusations against your brother. Peter and I had to control the situation, so we brought all three of them here."

"And me, too?"

"Exactly."

A kiss from Tobias to the center of Bethune's forehead confirmed a restored trust in his protector.

"Come, Tobias. Let's fill our bellies. Then, I will fill my belly with you."

A light-hearted wrestling match ensued, which led to Frederick having his appetizer first. They finished their meal, buried themselves beneath the coverings and snuggled in darkness. Tobias and Frederick slept naked and content.

Being in good standing with Peter Sion did have its benefits, especially for two men as brave and clever as William Corder and Jonathan Sikes. After buckets of water were brought by the three assistants, a quick cleaning was done on both men in preparation for moving their activities elsewhere. It was quite a parade along the corridor leading from the torture chamber – William, with his arms draped over the shoulders of Sion and Otto for support; Jonathan, using Oscar and Herman in the same manner. They continued up the steps leading from the dungeon, along the hallway that passed the Chamber of Inquisition, and up another staircase taking them to the Grand Hall.

Sion glanced to the stairs leading to headquarters for the Bishop of

Grunewald. He long ago had figured out the whereabouts of Tobias. Having not seen the young man in the dungeon, nor having seen Frederick Bethune in the torture chamber, Peter Sion hoped that what he suspected was true and he smiled at the image of them together horizontally, somewhere up that staircase.

The generous living space devoted to Peter Sion was to the rear of the Grand Hall. The spacious rooms were all separate but connected by side doorways. They included his library, his dining hall, his sitting room and his bedroom – his and Otto's bedroom. Built into an outer wall to the left of the master's bed was a grand fireplace of mortared stone, and to the right of his bed, connected to the same room was a bathing area, equal in size to the bedroom itself.

Whereas under normal circumstances, man servants stationed in the nearby kitchen would tend to Sion's needs, this night was far from normal. Otto, Herman and Oscar would be performing that function. After laying William and Jonathan onto the bed, they began preparations for the bath. No mere tub this, it was a pit cut into the stone floor, oval in shape and ten feet in diameter. Kettles of fire-heated water were kept always at the ready off of the main kitchen and the three men, still naked and aromatic with dried-sweat, went there to retrieve this water.

The kitchen staff was startled when the three entered their area, but the appearance of Peter Sion calmed their fears. He made his dinner requests and helped his men load the kettles onto wheeled carts. As for William and Jonathan, they had immediately fallen into sleep upon touching the plush bedding and were unaware when the four men returned, despite the squeaking of their wheeled carts. Eight kettles of hot water were rolled to the edge of the pit and emptied.

"A few minutes of cooling will make the water tolerable." Sion used this time well. "Otto, we will make my potion here." Herman, you and Oscar see to the woman. Take some of this morning's bread from the kitchen. Lock her into a holding cell with bread and water, then return here."

Otto used one of the empty water kettles and hung it in the fireplace. All ingredients were kept in Sion's library, and as William and Jonathan continued their sleep, Peter and Otto made their goo.

When sitting on buttocks with legs in front, the water level in the bath came to the center of a man's chest. Jonathan and William were awakened and coaxed to sit there. They were joined by Peter, Oscar, Herman and Otto. None of the men bathed. They dunked their heads, surfaced, made themselves comfortable with backs against the wall, and slept... and slept... and slept.

It was a kitchen servant who awakened them. Peter commanded to the servant that their dinner was to be evenly distributed around the edge of the bath. Meats and vegetables were brought piled in heaps on huge platters. Each man had his own platter, with carafes of wine and steins of ale provided to wash it all down. As the entourage readied their meal, six men lathered and washed themselves. All remaining sweat, goo, semen and whatever else might be lingering upon hair and skin was soon circulating throughout the warm water where they sat.

Once everything was in place, Sion dismissed his staff, telling them he was not to be disturbed until he called for them. He exited the water, walked dripping to the double doors connecting bedroom to hallway and turned the lock.

The gathering of men took on the appearance of a council in water, with Sion re-assuming his place at one end of the oval, Jonathan to his right and in succession, William, Herman, Oscar and Otto. All six were famished and initially said little, as they devoured the food and drink surrounding them.

Once his belly was calmed a bit, Jonathan looked to Peter and spoke. "Should I not want to strangle you for what you did to me?"

"I suppose that is one option," Sion casually answered.

"I suppose I should try to stop you." William clasped his hand to the top of Jonathan's head and tousled his still-damp hair.

"Peter Sion, it seems as though William has taken a liking to you." Jonathan then pointed to the man opposite Sion. "Perhaps, instead, it is you who should be killed, Herman."

"I was good to you," Herman laughed. "You got only half of what I could give." He raised his arms and formed a U with arms and shoulders, flexing his chest, biceps and triceps. "Do you see this? I could have ruptured every organ, but Peter said no."

"Same for you, William." Oscar joined the conversation. "I could have ripped your limbs apart, but that was not Peter's intent."

"And why is that, Peter?" William asked.

"So you would display yourselves, especially Jonathan." He slipped his hand onto Jonathan's rapidly-filling-with-food belly and gave it a gentle squeeze. "Once I felt this hard wall, I just had to see your muscles in action."

Fully comfortable in the man's presence, Jonathan expanded his chest and tightened his belly for Sion's pleasure. "But, why the ruse?"

"What do you mean?"

"Why torture us? I would have done for you what I am doing now. You hold the power. I would have gladly offered myself to you."

Sion removed his hand. "I doubt that. Besides, how could I have known? You and William have concealed yourselves for many years. I don't know how, but you have."

None of the men, including Sion, could have known the wide-ranging scope of Frederick Bethune's six-year plot. Once Helena Sikes pulled the cord, the curtain rose and all of them were swept into this drama.

It was Oscar's foot making contact with William's foot that changed the subject. Soon, everything else was moot, because all six men were enjoying the pleasurable contacts of wet, soap-filmed skin. And as the fondling, kissing, massaging and squeezing continued, Sion exited the water to activate the drain. He reached down to take Otto's hand, dragging him away from the grasp of Jonathan's embrace. Together, they retrieved the kettle hanging above the bedroom fireplace fire and toted it to the pit, dumping its contents onto the stone floor.

The six men wallowed in the green, lubricating goo like lustful swine. They wrestled one another, changing partners and teaming up five against one, four against two, until their bodies were enveloped with Sion's stimulating potion. This was no common orgy. The stamina, strength and endurance of these men knew no bounds. Their heightened, ceaseless ecstasy defied words of description. No orgasm could calm their frenzied wanting for one another. No discharge into any orifice could tire their manly organs of sex. Only when their bodies collapsed from complete exhaustion did they sleep where they lay on the hard stone floor, mired in green muck.

Six healthy men slumbered in a tangled web. Six penises were fully charged and ready for action, but no energy remained for any of their owners to put them to good use.

The sun had just broken the horizon when Herman and Oscar removed themselves from the pit. With bodies rested and green potion still active, they returned to the dungeon and revisited Helena Sikes. Whatever was left of her was taken. Her weakened state no longer presented a threat from nails, fists or teeth. Besides, how could she resist them? These men were dominating brutes. Masculinity oozed from their pores. They smothered her with rock-hard muscle, manly fur and green goo. They invaded her ass, her vagina and her mouth, each man's cock visiting each hole as often as it wished. And when they were finally bored with her, they left Helena Sikes where she lay, a useless, sperm-filled rag mumbling crazed words of nonsense.

As for Peter, Otto and their guests, they moved to the private bath, where a modest-sized tub of hot water was waiting. One by one, they quickly removed the goo and drippings it had brought forth, then collapsed onto Sion's comfortable mattress. Peter's bed was more than enough size to accommode four sleeping men, provided they nestled together in pairs, two by two, Peter with his little bull, Jonathan with his beloved William. This bed was also conveniently sized for the activities when they awoke.

It was reassuring for Peter to know that these two men could perform just as easily without his potion, and that they gladly accepted him and Otto as their trusted friends. After all, William and Jonathan came from a different world, a world of secrecy and fear, whereas Peter and Otto lived in a world of power, where they could do whatever they wished.

They learned the hidden history of the two men from Grunewald, beginning with a replay of their first exploratory penis-to-anus encounter.

We were swimming in the Gasconade Stream," William explained. "Our wrestling in the water spilled onto the muddy bank. There was no thought to any of it. Was there, Jonathan?"

"No. We were both naked, caked with wet dirt and our dicks were hard."

"When Jonathan pinned me and laid on my back, I quit fighting. I could feel his penis wedged between my thighs and I squeezed them together."

"That was all the prodding I needed."

As Otto laid at the foot of the bed, crossways, just the same as when he had awaited Peter's awakening from his injury by boulder, Peter nestled behind him. He coaxed Otto to lay on his back with arms outstretched, so he could nestle between his legs instead. Peter's chest pressed Otto's penis and he used Otto's belly for a pillow.

It was his favorite pillow, for nothing could be so gorgeous as the stretched and flattened belly of his little bull.

Sion laid quietly on his pillow as Jonathan tenderly smothered William with his undulating muscles, William's chest on the mattress, Jonathan's chest on William's back. Peter alerted Jonathan to a jar of salve waiting on a bedside table, and he watched the two men complete their story.

Chapter two of their tale was a continuation of chapter one. Peter was shown how William first entered Jonathan, as he penetrated him from below. William laid on his back; Jonathan sat on his pole. Next, Jonathan moved from sitting to laying prone, with his back on top of William's chest. Jonathan tucked his hands beneath his own head, while William placed his hands onto Jonathan's thrust-into-the-air chest and massaged. His fingertips scraped across Jonathan's stretched nipples, which brought a pained moan from his throat.

"Uhhh... oh, my god... what are you doing to me?"

"Are you going to talk?" William asked from below.

"No, never."

Williams hands drifted onto Jonathan's belly and he dug his fingertips deep into the flattened muscle. "Talk, now, damn you."

"Never. You'll never break me."

Fantasies of torture, fantasies of erotic punishments, of dominance and submission, this is how the two had discovered one another.

William removed his hands from Jonathan and Peter Sion was allowed to partake of the muscled hero's stretched form. Otto was invited, but declined, preferring instead to reach for the salve. Peter put his tongue and lips to the powerful, expanded chest and hard, flattened belly of Jonathan, while William continued the questions and Jonathan continued the moans and words of defiance.

The invasion of the little bull's penis to Peter's backside culminated into Peter's mouth engulfing Jonathan's penis, which caused Jonathan's rectal wall to clinch and contort. The penis inside his rectum, that belonging to William, was crushed and stimulated by these contortions and both men were finished.

As in life outside the bedroom, Otto approached life inside the bedroom with the same confidence. He charged forward, grunting, growling and snorting droplets of mucus. He unleashed incredible bursts of strength with dominating thrusts and retractions the result. Otto was an unconquerable force no matter what endeavor he undertook, and if you can imagine the overwhelming power of a bull impaling your behind, then you can understand why Peter Sion clung to his little bull with every ounce of strength he could muster – both inside and outside the bedroom.

Their mid-afternoon breakfast was served on the bed, four men on their butts with knees bent, shins coming towards each other and ankles crossed.

"What do you men desire?"

Jonathan Sikes fielded Peter's question between bites of the first meal of the day.

"We wish to live without fear. We wish to be done with meetings in secret."

"You can do that here," Sion offered, after swallowing a morsel of pastry. "Here, you will be protected from all eyes. You will have access to anything or anyone you desire."

"No, sir, we are working men," William explained. "I am proud of my horses. Jonathan and his father tend the finest fields of wheat known. It is our pride. It defines us as men."

"Then, I will protect you from here. My men will be my eyes and ears, just as they are now."

"Why don't you make them your stewards?" Otto, always the strategist, joined in.

Peter never failed to listen. "How so?"

"Make them your liaisons between the castle and the village." Otto wiped his lips and fingers with linen cloth, so he could dramatize with masculine hands. "They can represent the villagers. They will having meetings, say, once a month and any requests the villagers have will be reported to you by Jonathan and William. In reverse, any information you need the villagers to know can be distributed by them."

"How does that protect them?" Peter was puzzled. "And how does it benefit me?"

"It will improve your relationship with the people. If they feel they are a part of Egbert Castle, they will work harder for Egbert Castle... more crops, higher-quality livestock."

"That's good for me. What about them?"

"They are commoners, working men, just like all people in Grunewald, but they represent you. Do you not think the people will respect them as your representatives? Do you not think the people will embrace their own kind collecting the necessary taxes and goods and information, as opposed to our soldiers, who treat them as though they are not human? You know how we are. We have no love for those who will not carry the sword."

"Hmm..." Peter was warming to the idea. "What do you men think?"

"I think it will work." Jonathan leapt from the mattress as another idea came to him. "We could appoint people under us to represent all of Grunewald... one for the field workers, one for the craftsmen, one for those who raise livestock."

"Good thought," Otto agreed. "Everybody will feel themselves to be a part of the realm."

It was a good thought in many ways, because with time, fear of Egbert Castle vanished. It became an extension of Grunewald and not a threat to its citizens. The people living in Peter Sion's realm adopted a sort of nationalism, desiring their kingdom to be better than all others. And because the people were busy improving their lot, soldiers and spies were no longer necessary. Any troublemakers were immediately reported to their representatives, who passed the information to Jonathan and William, who passed it along to Peter Sion for his consideration. At Otto's suggestion, Peter was able dispatch more soldiers to patrol his borders and better protect outlying settlements, which is what soldiers should do and would prefer to do.

And so, all plans were finalized in the master's bedroom, but not implemented until the next day. This is because William and Jonathan remained in the bed of Peter and Otto for the remainder of that afternoon and evening, further consecrating their partnerships in the village of Grunewald and in Egbert Castle.

This, too, was the sole activity of Frederick Bethune and Tobias Corder. The young man was a ceaseless fountain, an attribute to which all men of eighteen years can lay claim. Their conversations between fornications offered Tobias that world in his dream. Rather than aspiring to the mundane occupation of a blacksmith, he agreed with Frederick that the life of a Bishop brought greater rewards. With mentor, protector and lover by his side, Tobias apprenticed to become the future Bishop of Grunewald – a training which involved world travels with Frederick and access to the finest foods, clothing, jewels and all other things promised to him.

Interest in and involvement with the people of Grunewald became more church-like for Frederick. His meddlesome days were no more, his sole interest, Tobias.

William could offer no protest. What better way for him to release

Tobias from his mother-smothering, brotherly love? With a mind-set tuned to everyone's happiness, William Corder gifted his brother to the care of Frederick Bethune, never again admonishing Tobias for anything he wished to do.

As days passed, the interaction between Frederick and Peter was limited to official need. Frederick was consumed with Tobias and Peter with Otto. Neither the Bishop nor Tobias had any interest in the lure of the torture chamber. Everything they could ever want was centered around themselves in the headquarters built by Egbert Sion for the Bishop of Grunewald

Frederick did eventually dispatch the proper papers to Rome for the disposal of Helena Sikes. In an open courtyard within the castle walls, seen by no one besides Peter Sion when he desired to look, the wretched woman was tied naked to a horizontal, wooden beam that extended from the outer stone wall supporting Sion's bedroom. With her wrists roped to the beam, she dangled, suspended in midair. Her only views were the stone walls surrounding her and a monument devoted to a sorceress, the only female for whom Peter Sion had ever shown reverence.

Surely by the fourth day she had repented to no one but herself and God, for on the fifth day her life on this earth was no more. Only her corpse remained, the flesh rotting to leave nothing but bones, which eventually collapsed to a heap on the ground.

As he did every morning, Peter stood at his bedroom window, glancing quickly to the grey-skinned corpse before eyeing his monument and paying his respects. As his meditation ended, a puff of hot air hit the back of his neck.

"Why do you snort, Otto?"

Two massive forearms and a powerful chest squeezed Peter in their vise. "It is time for your son to become a king."

Peter clasped his hands onto the furred forearms pressing his chest.

"I know this. I have been procrastinating."

"And I know why."

"Of course you do. It is a beginning for him... an ending for us."

"Not really. Just a return to where we started."

Peter turned to face him. "Will you teach him the ways of a soldier?"

"Gladly. I will return to live with Oscar and Herman. Your son will know me only as a soldier."

"The finest ever to be."

"And so will he be."

As William and Jonathan enjoyed their freedom, Peter and Otto relinquished theirs. The future king and his sisters were brought to live in rooms off of the Grand Hall, but Otto did not rejoin his brother and his cousin in their dungeon quarters. As instructor of soldierly duties, Otto was headquartered near the future king, and also near the current king. They seized opportunities of togetherness when they could. More often than not, those opportunities came easier in the torture chamber.

The bedroom, when available, was for love, but Peter further practiced his religion by using the Board of Impalement, Steps to Purgatory and other implements of torture. They became props – the alters upon which he worshiped his god – namely, Otto – and on occasion Herman and Oscar.

Age of enlightenment? It was a beginning. No need for torture? Only for fantasy, which in actuality had been the only purpose of the torture chamber since the ungodly death of the bandit, Thomas Gavin. After Otto had saved him from his madness, Peter saw his torture chamber as a theater of lust – a festival of masculine grunts, groans, smells, muscle and semen.

Jonathan and William would often revisit the torture chamber to play out their fantasies as well. Everybody was converted to Peter's religion. Entire days and nights were spent with each man taking his turn as tortured hero. Herman, Otto and Oscar joined them and one man at a time would allow himself to be bound to a device of his choosing. Once bound, he would receive the praise of the other five. Sometimes potion was used, sometimes not, but by perfecting Peter's religion, these six men soon forgot about females altogether. After all, who knows better the proper ways to please a man's penis than a man who owns one himself?

Tank Books

Epilogue
A Few Words from Otto

Peter never asked me about my five day absence following the Battle of Runyan Bridge, but I told him anyway. I waited until we both sported white hair and Peter was laying on his bed in preparation of leaving me. He was afraid to leave me... kept mumbling about how he would be lost without me and that only I could protect him and on and on, until I told him to be quiet and listen to my story.

Bernard's men found me naked and they tortured me naked. Frankly, I don't know why they bothered. I didn't have any information and they didn't need any, but they had figured out I was the man who destroyed the bridge, so I guess it was just a way for them to get revenge against me... before my execution. That is why they brought in Bernard's daughter to watch. It is also the moment I knew there was a chance for me.

She violently attacked me, as I laid helplessly bound to their stretch rack. Their rack was simple in comparison to ours... our beloved Steps to Purgatory... their rack was just a narrow, horizontal table with axles at both ends and plenty of rope wound around each of them. Both of their axles had hand cranks and one man turned the head end one direction, while another turned the foot end another direction.

Elsa entered the room in a rage. She pounded my chest with her fists, screaming of how I had killed her father and how she would enjoy watching me suffer. And I did suffer. I thanked the heavens for the muscles provided me, for only they could keep my body together.

Despite Elsa's ferocious demeanor, I saw in her eyes... when she leaned over me with her pounding fists... I saw in her eyes a softness for me. As she flailed on my helpless body, her eyes scanned my body from feet to hands and the severity of her fists lessened. She probably didn't realize it, but I did.

So, when the men resumed my stretching and I grunted and groaned and flexed to resist the ropes, my mind focused on you... I hardly knew you, but still, my mind was focused on you, Peter... and my penis focused on you, Peter... and the only weapon available to me was used against her because of you, Peter. And when Elsa saw my penis rise and flip onto my belly, despite my stretching, despite the ungodly pain racking my body, I knew she was mine.

Elsa is the one who demanded my execution take place immediately and they released me from the rack. They took me to an open courtyard inside their castle walls and roped me to a cross of wood, the same kind the Romans used... the same kind Frederick slobbers over. Once I was vertical, a new kind of pain racked my body. The pressure of weight bearing on my arms was ungodly and it was all I could do to breath, but I held on... and I waited... until everyone became bored and I was all alone.

And when Elsa arrived, secretly, her head covered by an oversized hood, my penis was ready... thanks to you, Peter.

There's no way to describe the sensation of oral stimulation on my penis as I hung from the cross. My brain was deprived of oxygen and I think this put me into a sort of dream state, but I do know this... Elsa was overwhelmed by what the gods had bestowed on me, because it was she that arranged my rescue, after efficiently draining my cock.

And the only real purpose of her arranging my descent and release from the cross was so she could feel that same penis inside her. And she did feel me inside her... inside her vagina, and her anus and her mouth again. Four times I dominated her... once from the cross... three times in her bed and each time it was because of you, Peter.

It is true what you say. I am an unconquerable force. The gods have decreed it. Elsa could not bear the thought of my execution, not after what I had done to her. She took me to the River Runyan herself, she and her servants. She took me to a place in the river where I could swim to you, Peter, so don't think you are ever leaving me, because you can't. I think I have proven that time and again.

Wherever you're going, just wait... your little bull will join you and nothing will stop him.

Tank Books

OUR BETTING GAME
How two young men discover
their sexuality

God, I was pissed. Here I was grounded again, sitting alone on a Sunday afternoon, forbidden to go anywhere besides the empty playground at my old school, Woodrow Wilson Elementary. My mom, the bloodhound, had once again sniffed out the vapors from my Saturday night drinking. Two sips from a bottle of cheap wine and I was caught. Obviously, I wasn't drunk. I'd done everything in my power to prevent this from happening, but when you're out with your buddies and everyone else is having sips, you've got to partake.

Funny, they could always get away with it, and I'd do everything in my power to do the same. I'd eat red hots, breath mints, a hamburger with raw onions and smoke cigarettes, but nothing worked. I always came home on time and never did anything rowdy, but mom was fervently against alcohol and would begin grilling me as soon as I came through the door. She always knew. She had given up on stopping me from smoking, but alcohol would not be tolerated in any quantity.

So, to get away from the tension in the house, I'd always ask if I could walk the few blocks to my old haunts. The school was close to the railroad tracks and I'd just sit, smoke and watch the occasional train rumble past. Or in between, I'd blankly stare at the empty swings and merry-go-round, the spring breeze gently setting them in motion.

As I sat on the sidewalk next to the building and gazed down the grassy hill towards our playground, I was thinking about some of my old pals from those days, the games we'd play, climbing the jungle gym or just running across the open field to the baseball diamond. Most of them I hardly knew now. We had all drifted apart, as we progressed to the big junior high and even bigger high school. Now we were all seniors and had made new friends along the way. I wondered if any of them had the same earth-shattering problems as I did. Man, I was really PISSED!

My spirits were lifted a bit by the sudden appearance of my friend Thomas, who came whizzing around the corner on his ten-speed bike. He buzzed past me, calling out my name using his mocking, effeminate voice.

"M a r k i e!"

He took off down the hill, circled the swing sets and headed back for me. His strong legs bulged as he pumped the pedals, powering the bike back uphill without needing to downshift. He was always showing off that way and I always egged him on. We'd been friends for four years, having met in a freshman English class and discovering we were both crazy about rock music, more specifically, The Who.

He returned to the sidewalk and nudged his front wheel against my shoulder. This time he taunted me with that famously sarcastic melody, "Markie got grounded, Markie got grounded!"

"What the hell are you doing here?"

Thomas smiled, "I thought we'd go bike riding, but your mom said you were in the doghouse again for drinking."

"Yeah, I gotta stay home or I can come here, that's it."

"For how long?"

"'Til a week from today. Did you ride all the way over here?" Thomas lived almost 15 miles from my house, which was no big deal to him. He used to come over on his bike all the time before we could drive. I just wondered why he didn't drive over today. "Where's the car?"

"I'm grounded, too, at least as far as my parents' car is concerned. I kinda had a little fender-bender last night."

"No shit? What happened?"

"Me and Kevin were just cruising around looking for something to do. Do you know that big doofus Randy Crane?"

"Yeah, I know he's an asshole."

"Well, him and a carload..."

"He and a carload..."

"Up yours! Ok. He and a carload of his goofball friends pull up next to us at a red light. They start yelling out shit like me and Kevin are queer, you know. So I told 'em all to go get fucked, and when the light changed, one of 'em threw a soda can and hit the car. Crane takes off and I started chasing him. Man, we went flying down Monroe Avenue like crazy. I never even looked at the speed. So he turns on 16th street and I'm right behind him. You know how 16th jogs when it crosses Washington? Well, that's where I got hit. This car on Washington clipped my back fender and spun me around. It was no big deal, nobody got hurt. Kevin was laughing his ass off. So anyway, the cops came and I had 'em call my dad and that was it."

"How long are you grounded?"

"They didn't say. I guess until they get over it. I tell you one thing, I'm gonna kick that mother fucker's ass when I see him."

Thomas could easily do just that. He was an athletic nut, and besides that, his dad boxed when he was in the Navy and had shown all his kids the sweet science. I had seen Thomas lay out a guy twice his size back when we first met.

A left hook to the ribs and straight right to the center of the guy's chest. He fell like a big oak tree being chopped down, BAM, flat on his back and never got up. It was a thing of beauty, watching my little freshman pal down the big, bad senior.

"I can't wait to see you do it to him. He's needed an ass kicking for a long time."

Thomas loved to hear me throw accolades his way, especially when it had to do with his athletic abilities. He beamed as he stepped off the bike and secured it with the kick stand. Standing beside me, he lowered himself and crossed his legs Indian-style to sit facing me and to my right.

"So, how do you feel? Does your head hurt?"

"I only took two little drinks. My mom can smell me every time no matter what I do."

I scooted to my right and crossed my legs like his so we could be face to face. When I did, my dick fell out of the cutoff jean shorts I was wearing. Having been in a foul mood, I hadn't bothered to put on underwear that day. I was unaware of what had happened, but Thomas' uncontrolled laughter told me something was up.

"Man, put that thing away!" He was staring at my crotch. "You're scaring the hell out of me, you pervert."

I looked down to see the head of my weenie sticking out from the fringe of the cutoffs. I casually tucked it back in and scowled at him, "Don't worry, he's no threat today. He's mad at the world just like I am."

"Hey, if you're gonna get caught anyway, why not just go all out and get smashed?" Thomas was still smiling from my pud's attempted escape.

"Oh, hell, I don't really even like it that much. I just do it because it's there and everyone else is drinking it. You know, when they offer me the bottle, what am I supposed to say?"

"Bullshit! You love it and you know it. You're lucky your mom stops you. Otherwise, you'd get drunk every day."

Now, he knew this wasn't true, but this was a game we'd play.

"No way. I'm finished with it. Next time I'm just telling them I don't want any. I'm tired of going through this crap with her." I had set the table for him and I knew what was next.

"You liar! I'll bet you can't go without a drink until we graduate. That's about six weeks away and I bet you can't do it."

So the betting game was begun. Thomas would always bet that I couldn't do something, usually involving my brain, that he knew I could do. And I in return would bet that he couldn't do something athletic, when I knew full well that he could.

My ambition was to see him do something physical. His ambition was to show me how physical he was, which is why he always got to start the game.

Now it was my turn to challenge him. "All right, I'll take that bet, but I'll bet you can't climb those two poles with just your hands." I pointed to one of the basketball goals, which was supported by two metal poles coming from the ground three feet apart.

Thomas jumped up to his feet. "Piece of cake!" He mounted his bike and I followed him down the hill.

This is why we were such great pals. He admired my brain and I admired his body. Our friendship started because of our mutual need of one another. Back in that freshman English class, one of our first assignments was to write an argument and orally present it before the class. Mine was why Pete Townshend was one of the greatest guitarists and songwriters ever. Like I said, this is how we first hooked up. But more importantly, without me, Thomas never would have passed that class, nor any other language classes through four years of high school.

As for what he meant to me, I was a puny weakling when I was in ninth grade. Thomas saved me from many bloody noses and other injured body parts. Once the word got out that I was his buddy, no bullies ever bothered me again. My junior year I began to fill out and Thomas had shown me a few tricks from the boxing game, so I no longer really needed him to protect me, but I still needed him as my friend. I was always there to answer his questions about school work and I enjoyed helping him.

Thomas was not arrogant about his physique. He was naturally powerful and never needed to work too hard to keep it that way. But he liked to show his upper body to me. He felt comfortable in my presence and enjoyed accepting any challenge I threw his way. I had never once asked him to remove his shirt, he just always did it - for me.

So here he was with his shirt gone and one hand on each pole. I was standing right in front of him. He began to climb, moving one hand at a time higher. As soon as his feet left the ground, I was in awe. His dark green gym shorts were set about two inches below his navel, and as he climbed they started to inch even lower. I could clearly see every line of his powerful chest and abdominals, as they strained to assist the arms lift him higher a few inches at a time. Soon, his legs were at my eye level. Absolutely gorgeous they were, even though he wasn't really using them. Hair had just started to grow on his thighs, whereas the shins and calves were handsomely furry, not curly q's, just thick, straight and short brown hairs. He wore white unstriped socks that he himself had kind of pushed down into wrinkles, leaving them about five inches above his black Converse All Stars.

This challenge was so easy for him. He almost glided up the poles, as he looked up to the basketball goal to gauge the distance left for him. I loved watching his arms. Both biceps and triceps worked in harmony like fine-tuned machines, magically lifting him up towards the goal. Soon he proclaimed his triumph, "Did it!"

"Oh, by the way, did I mention you have to come down the same way?"

"No problem." And my magnificent Thomas began his descent towards me one hand at a time. As his ankles got back to my waist, he stopped to issue the next challenge. "Bet you can't pull me off of here."

"Oh yeah?" I grabbed each ankle and started to tug.

"Wait a second." I let up on him and Thomas adjusted the position of his hands to get a better grip. "Ok. Now."

I pulled with all my might. Gazing up at his beautiful body, I could see it all. His thighs were even with my forehead. The gym shorts had drifted down to just above his pubic hair and his beautiful belly muscles were stretched as tight as they could be. A thin line of hair connected his belly button to the pubes, tantalizingly hidden under his shorts. That glorious chest of his was flexed and expanded to capacity, every masculine line of power clearly defined for me to relish. He gritted his teeth and clenched his jaw, displaying his rugged determination to defeat me in this challenge.

My triceps were getting sore and I decided to cheat. I wrapped my arms around the back of his knees and pressed my body against the front. Then I bent my knees, lifting my feet off the ground and adding all of my weight to his stretching. This did not faze him one bit. He continued to grasp the poles and hang suspended, as though I wasn't even there. Thomas groaned and mocked me in a manly voice. "You cheater! Do what you must. None of your tortures will break me."

That statement nearly drove me nuts. I came so close to burying my face into his gym shorts that I don't know what stopped me. Perhaps, I was afraid that such a move would end our game forever, which I was enjoying way too much. I did not want to take that risk. I held on with all my strength and turned my head to the side, just so I would not be tempted by the sight of his glorious physique.

Finally, he wore me out. I lowered my feet to the ground and released him. "Ok, ok. You are too strong. You win this one."

Thomas remained suspended on the poles. "That's right, I am, and don't you forget it." He descended the poles to complete his triumph, one hand at a time until he returned to earth.

Now I had a problem. Since it had been allowed to roam free, my dick was again poking out of the leg of my shorts, but this time it was hard as a rock. I quickly told him I had to piss, turned and ran for the bushes near the railroad tracks. Once there, I unzipped and pretended to pee, then put willie back in the center and pointing up towards my belly button. I zipped up the shorts and safely covered the entire mess with my white pocket t-shirt.

That problem temporarily resolved, I returned to the basketball goal, where Thomas was pacing with hands on hips, still breathing heavily from his victory. Most guys would have pulled their shorts back up to where they wanted them, but not Thomas. He left them right there above the pelvic bone, just so I could see every inch of his rippling abdominals. I hadn't yet decided where the game should go next, so I switched subjects. "Too bad you didn't call first. Would have saved you a trip over here. Wish I could go bike riding with you."

He stood under the goal and again placed his hands on the poles above his head. Then, he leaned forward, stretching out his chest and belly as he yawned, "I did call."

My peter was doing everything in its power to get out of those cutoffs, but it was locked safely in place running up the inside of the zipper line. God damn him, I loved it so much when he taunted me with his body. He didn't do it to be cruel. It was just his way of showing how comfortable he felt around me, a confidence in our friendship. Thomas didn't know any more about my leanings than I did in those days.

We had both turned 18, but for some reason, when Thomas and I were together, we both had the mind set of post-puberty 14 year olds. Hanging out with my other friends, I'd act more like an adult, and I'm sure Thomas did too. But the two of us together and alone would try to hang on to that youth, playing our challenge game and preserving our innocence.

"You mean you knew I was grounded and rode all the way over here anyway?"

"Yeah, I figured you could use some cheering up."

That was so Thomas. The guy would do about anything for me and I never really understood why. Maybe it was because we were as different as cats and dogs. What I didn't know, he'd teach me and vice versa. We bonded right from the start when we were 14 years old, especially the first time he came over to spend the night.

My bedroom was in the basement far removed from everyone else in the house. No one could get near my closed door without me knowing it. After the lights were out, Thomas and I began the usual boyhood conversations in the dark, as we lay on our backs and separated, each on our own side of my full size bed. One of my first comments was that Pete Townshend's music gave me a hard-on. Thomas agreed and then asked a question that stunned me. "Why do dicks do that?"

"What do you mean?"

"What makes them get big like that? Sometimes mine starts to grow and I don't know why."

I couldn't believe the poor guy was still in the dark about this. I knew his father was a strict disciplinarian, but some things you just learn on your own. "Dicks get hard so we can fuck and make babies."

"So that's where we stick it in them like those lions do on National Geographic?"

I tried not to laugh. "Well, there's a little more to it than that, but basically, yes. Difference is, we're supposed to kiss and make love to them, so they'll get all horny before we shoot our load into them. We're not supposed to bite them on the neck like lions do. Most girls don't like that."

Thomas jumped right in with curiosity. "Now, I've heard that before. Shoot your load. What the hell does that mean?"

I couldn't believe this poor guy. "Have you ever jacked off?"

"Well, one time I was laying in bed and my peter got big. For whatever reason I reached down and put my finger on top of it. Then I kind of rubbed it and, before I knew it, this warm gooey crap was all over my belly. It scared the hell out of me. My room was dark and I couldn't see what it was, so I just grabbed some Kleenex and wiped it all off and went to sleep."

I had to chuckle. I just couldn't help myself. "Well Thomas, that night you jacked off and didn't even know it. I remember the first time I did that was sort of the same way. Have you ever done it again?"

"Nope. I'm afraid to."

"Oh, hell. It's perfectly natural. That sperm that came out on your belly is what mixes with the egg inside a woman to make babies. There's a whole bunch of different ways to do it. You wanna try?"

"Sure. I mean, it did feel good, I just didn't know what it was."

"Well, here. I'll show you what to do."

I got up and lit a candle on the table at my bedside, then I pulled the covers back to his knees.

"Get your feet out here and take off your underwear." Thomas obediently did as he was told, while I dropped my shorts, revealing my already erect penis. "Look Thomas, just thinking about jacking off has got me hard."

He glanced over and quickly returned his eyes to the ceiling. I got back on the bed and looked at his naked form. He was scared shitless, hands at his sides and every muscle tensed. His penis lay comfortably in between the testicles like an egg on a nest, legs clamped close together.

"Now, put your hand around your dick and close your eyes. Start thinking about something that turns you on, like someone you know or some movie star that you find attractive."

Thomas wrapped his right hand around the shaft and closed his eyes.

"Squeeze your dick and pump it, relax and then squeeze."

He started pumping his unit, but nothing was happening. He was so uptight that it wouldn't respond. I couldn't believe the guy wasn't getting a hard-on. Hell, at this time of my life my cock had a mind of its own, getting erect whether I was thinking about anything hot or not. All I had to do was touch it.

So I had to coax him. "Thomas, relax. Spread your legs out a little so your balls can breathe. Let your mind go, take a deep breath and try to remember how good it felt that time you got off."

I actually was enjoying his struggle. This time allowed me to admire my new friend's perfect body, the flickering candle casting a warm glow on his smooth skin. I really wanted to caress his gorgeous chest and belly to help him out, but better judgment stopped me. Slowly, but surely, Thomas got his erection.

"Look over here a second." He opened his eyes to see what I was doing. I laid back down and began to stroke my eight-incher. "Start moving your hand like this and put your finger over the head right here. Can you see this?"

Thomas raised up enough to see what I was doing. "Yeah, I think I got it."

"Good. Now lay back down, close your eyes and jack that baby off."

And away we went. I wanted to finish first so bad, just so I could watch him go. I had only got a glimpse of his unit in its erect state. It was about seven inches, nice thickness and cut. A real pretty cock to go with his beautiful bod. Every now and then I'd sneak a peak, opening my left eye to watch him stroke. Even at this young age, his pectorals were well-developed and puffing up from excitement. I could see his nipples becoming more and more firm, the tips getting longer and starting to point. He began sucking in his belly, that heavenly, hard line of muscle, still hairless and firm as a rock. I don't know what he was thinking about and I didn't care. The natural masculine beauty of my new friend sent me to orgasm in no time. Neither of us made a sound except for our rapid breathing. My initial spurt shot up and hit me under the chin, then the following contractions left a dotted trail of sperm all the way down my chest. Finally, several more gobs formed a pool in my navel before I was totally spent. I laid there gasping and turned my head to watch him work it.

His pace was increasing. I saw his fingers changing positions, as he explored the places where his big round poker was most sensitive. He perfected his method and tightened every beautiful muscle.

"Oh, my god." Thomas whispered a warning before his eruption. I don't even know where his first explosion went. I saw it come out, but it went somewhere past his face to the headboard beyond.

I watched in amazement as subsequent shots of cum peppered his upper torso, landing everywhere on his chest, stomach and belly. Thomas continued to stroke, as he arched his back and writhed in uncontrolled pleasure. The last contractions oozed huge spurts onto his belly button, filling it to the rim and overflowing, making a circle the size of a Kennedy half dollar.

Poor Thomas. His balls must have been building up sperm for untold months, but thanks to me, they would suffer no more.

He opened his eyes and looked over to me with a boyish grin. "That was fucking great. I can't believe how good that felt. Thank you, Mark, I will never forget this."

I reached over and got the Kleenex, setting the box in between us. "Now you know why our dicks get hard."

After the cleanup, our conversation returned to the mundane until we finally fell asleep. Of course, we did it again in the morning while it was still dark, and every other time we had sleep overs. It just became our thing to do. Thomas was the only one I did this with, and it eventually became part of our betting game - who could shoot the biggest load or who could get off the most times. It got to where we didn't sleep much at night because we were obsessed with jacking off together.

We never discussed what we were thinking about when we beat off. In fact, neither of us ever talked about girls when we were together, even when we had both started dating them. When Thomas and I were alone, we were only interested in ourselves and each other.

Back in those days, I never thought of myself as homosexual. I didn't really even know or care what that was. Once I got my driver's license, I went on several dates where I'd give a poke to the babe of the evening in the back seat of the car and thought nothing of it. Hell, that's what a boy was supposed to do and I never had any trouble performing.

But Thomas created a problem. For whatever reason, every time I was around him I'd get a big hard-on, and he was the only guy who had ever effected me this way. When we were beating off it was ok because I had a legitimate reason, but any other time I would have to be ready for him.

My solution was to wear a jock strap a size too small. I know it sounds painful and sometimes it was, but this kept my big dick hidden from him. In public I didn't have to worry, but at his house or my house, this was mandatory. I knew he would always want to wrestle or do something to impress me with his body, and I could not allow him to see my reaction.

One time he asked me why I always wore a strap, but I had prepared for this. I told him my dick always wanted to flop to the left, but I liked it on the right, and a jock strap held it in place. He thought I was pretty clever to come up with that idea. Once again, he loved my brain and I loved his brawn.

Thomas was not a show off. I don't even think he knew how beautiful he was. Whether he was in gym class or wrestling practice, he never removed his shirt or displayed himself to anyone until he had to shower. He only did that around me. I guess he could sense that I enjoyed him, and as a way of thanking me for our friendship and all that I had taught him, he loved to exhibit his manly athleticism for my eyes only.

Today he had caught me off guard. Not only was I without my jock strap, I didn't even have any friggin' underwear. And now here we were in the middle of our challenge game, his open invitation to show me his glorious body, and it was my turn.

"I'm glad you came over. You did cheer me up."

Thomas stepped closer and puffed up his chest. "That's great tough guy, but what have you got for me now?"

And so he wanted another challenge. Well, so did I. "I bet I can shoot a wad before you can."

My pal was not expecting this and he stepped back. "You mean here, out in the open?"

"Sure, why not? There's nobody around."

I had really thrown him a curve this time. We had never done this anywhere but in my bedroom.

"I don't think that's too cool."

"So you're declining my challenge?"

"I don't know, man. What if someone shows up? We could get arrested."

"Ok, I'll give you a break. Let's go down there by the tracks. No one will see us, except maybe an engineer if a train goes by."

My big man was still a little uneasy. "I don't know if we should. The train guy could radio the police."

I knew what would get him - mock chicken sounds, "bok, bok, bok, bok," as I pretended to flap my wings. "Come on, man. Railroad guys aren't gonna give a shit. Even if they do see us, they'll probably just think it's funny. Bok, bok, bok."

"Ok pal, you're on. You're gonna lose, too. Last night was a bust. I didn't even jack it after all that happened with my wreck."

"Get your bike and let's go. No one will even know we're down there."

So off we went, down towards the tracks. Bushes and trees would hide us from the school yard and I found us a place where the railroad guys wouldn't see us either. We were about 20 yards from the tracks, surrounded by chest-high bushes and massive black walnut trees. All the growth was lush and green. Thomas parked the bike and draped his shirt over the seat. He looked around at the environment I had chosen and decided he was comfortable. "Are we gonna strip?"

"Hell yes!"

It felt so good to set my hard dick free. Thomas was not concerned because he knew my cock always got hard when we were going to jack off. We stood facing each other two feet apart and he gazed at my big unit. "Looks like you're getting a head start on me. Are you ready?"

"Does it look like it?"

He burst out laughing, "Slightly!"

I gave the signal, "Ready? GO!"

Now I saw him in all his glory, in the daylight totally naked. The beautiful boy was now a manly man. I looked at his masculine feet, strong tendons raised along the instep, small tufts of brown hair on his great toes. My eyes moved up to his ankles, a strong connection to those gorgeous, hairy shins and calves. Precision engineered knee caps led up to his powerful thighs, just now beginning to sprout little hairs. I never realized the thick beauty of his pubic hair, golden brown and sparkling in the sunlight. I skipped past the hand clutching and stroking his penis, only because I wanted to focus on that powerful belly with the precious, newly sprouted fur trail connecting his manhood to the navel. He was struggling a bit to get a hard-on, and he had his abdomen flexed in an attempt to get it going. This drove me nuts. What a glorious sight it was, firm muscles rippling from the rib cage to pelvic bone, a handsomely oval belly button, deeply inset and melding with those powerful abdominals to form a masterpiece of design. And now the chest. Gorgeous beyond description, his fully developed pectorals flexed and bulged as he jacked his meat. And parked firmly underneath each pec, those perfectly rounded nipples pointed down, slowly becoming smaller, forcing the tips to lengthen as his excitement grew.

Too late. The sight of Thomas's incredible masculinity brought me to orgasm before I even knew what was happening. I pointed my dick down so I wouldn't shoot all over him. Do I need to tell you that I made a big white puddle of cum on the ground?

"Jesus Christ, man! How long you been saving it up?"

"I got off this morning. What the hell are you talking about?"

"Bullshit. That's one of the biggest loads I ever saw you shoot. Do hangovers always make you have big goobers like that?"

"I don't have a hangover, you smart-ass. You just can't handle being around a real man." I was relishing this banter. Thomas didn't know that he was the reason for my superiority in this challenge.

"Oh yeah, big man? Well, I bet you can't suck my dick without gagging."

Holy shit, did he really say that? Now it was my turn to step back. I looked Thomas in the eye. He was giving me that boyish grin that I first saw the night I taught him how to jack off. His eyes flashed down to his erect penis and my eyes followed. He had stopped stroking it and now he was protruding before me as hard as could be. I could see the blood pumping in the veins of the organ, and it bobbed up each time his heart beat.

Obviously, Thomas had figured out that he was the reason I could get off so fast. He had been wanting to issue this challenge for years, and now he had finally found the right moment.

"You're on, punk." I knelt before him and took his penis into my mouth. At first I was a little apprehensive, afraid that I would gag on him. I toyed with the head and played around on it using my tongue. Then I got brave. My mouth was accommodating me with plenty of saliva, so I moved my lips slowly down his shaft. Eventually I reached the base of his penis and I held him prisoner. Wrapping my tongue on the underside of the throbbing shaft, I pressed my lips into his pubic hair and squeezed the bulging mushroom head in my throat. Thomas groaned and began massaging his chest and belly. He worked his hands all around that glorious torso, eventually reaching for and rubbing his erect nipples. Then he put his hands behind his head and arched his back, thrusting his penis forward and offering it up for me to worship.

Seeing him in this pose was too much. I was now fully confident in myself and I drew my lips slowly away, lingering and working my tongue on the head of his dick before releasing him.

Thomas raised his hands towards the sky and stretched. Then he looked down at me and yawned as he spoke, "Well, now what?"

"I didn't gag, I win."

"You didn't get me off, you don't win."

I had everything I wanted, but I was not satisfied. "Ok, tough guy. We'll have a double challenge. I'll bet you can't get off while hanging from that tree limb." I pointed to where I wanted him to go.

"Are you going to suck me?"

"Hell yes."

"That's no challenge. You know I'll get off."

"Your challenge isn't much either. You know I'll get you off."

"You're on." Thomas ran to the tree and waited for me. He looked up to the horizontal branch, then raised his arms towards it and smiled at me. "Lift me up."

What a sweetheart. Thomas could easily have jumped up and latched on, but he wanted me to do it. I clasped my hands on his powerful laterals, strategically placing my thumbs on the nipples, and boosted him upwards. He grabbed the branch and waited for me, toes three inches from the ground, penis hard and ready to spit in my eye.

I engulfed him. Immediately, I pressed my lips into that golden pubic hair and squeezed his dick in my throat. Like the rest of him, his cock was absolutely perfect. It wasn't until years later, after I had established myself as a world-class cock sucker, that I realized just how perfect his penis really was. I have serviced guys with sloppy foreskins, peters that bent in the middle, some so thick I couldn't help them and some so tiny I couldn't find them. Thomas' dick was custom made for sucking on. Like I said before, he was seven inches and cleanly circumcised. The diameter was just right for engulfing with lips and tongue, one and a half inches. And the shape of the mushroom head was exactly what a mouth needs to provide maximum stimulation to a man without breaking one's jaw.

I slowly drew back my lips and began to work him over. Keeping my hands free, I methodically and slowly moved back and forth on his shaft. My tongue gently massaged the underside as I orally stroked him. Each time my lips approached the rim of his mushroom, I'd lovingly wrap my tongue underneath and mercilessly lick this most sensitive spot. Keeping my lips firmly clamped at all times, saliva was conveniently providing the necessary lubricant for me to properly service my manly god.

I gazed up to Thomas' face. His head was erect and facing forward, but his eyes were closed. Other than his breathing, he made no sounds. I was taking his mind some place he wanted to go, and I sensed where that place might be. I grabbed each of his ankles and pulled down to gently stretch him. Thomas groaned and flexed his powerful body, keeping his eyes closed. Now he shared his fantasy with me.

"Go ahead, torture me all you want. I will never be broken."

My own dick was begging to be stroked, but I was too busy. As I continued to service him at a slightly quicker pace, I looked up to take in all his glory. He had extended the lower jaw while his mouth and eyes were still closed. His belly was sucked in and chest expanded, striking a pose of rugged and manly defiance. Again he verbalized a challenge to his imaginary tormentors.

"None of your chains or bizarre tortures will break me. I am too strong for all of you."

A distant sound drifted through the air, clearly the horn of a diesel locomotive. I increased the tempo on Thomas' throbbing penis. Ever so slowly, I tugged with more pressure on his ankles and watched him lift up his toes to arch those manly feet. Sporadically, I'd slide my hands down over the tops of his feet, continuing on to caress the arched soles underneath. Then I'd wrap my thumbs over the tops and curl my fingernails into his masculine arches, lightly scratching the soles of his feet. Thomas threw back his head as his pretend agony worsened.

"You bastards, I will never talk. No torture can break me."

The train got closer and ground started to shake, but nothing could bring Thomas or me back to reality. For more than three years our orgasms had been separate entities, but now we were conjoined. Our mutual jack offs and challenges had prepared us for this event, which neither of us knew was coming. I sensed our closeness and transferred the overwhelming admiration I had for him onto his penis. My oral worship of him became something undescribable. I knew what made my dick feel good, and I communicated all of this knowledge to the cock of my magnificent Thomas.

He felt the reverberations I was sending up his shaft. Like a boomerang, he absorbed the sensations and sent them back to me. I felt the organ in my mouth grow harder and more powerful than any penis could possibly be. Like the increasing vibrations from the approaching train, a resounding unification of the worshiped and the worshiper made the ground beneath us tremble. Everything I felt for Thomas and everything he felt for me had come together, right where his manhood met my mouth. I tugged at his ankles to stretch him just a little more.

Clamping harder with my jaw, I tightened the pressure on his cock, all the while stroking him with my lips and tongue.

I gazed up at this perfect specimen of masculinity to see him smiling at me, his eyes glazed with total ecstasy. The train was here and the engineer blasted that deafening air horn. I saw Thomas mouth those words he whispered on our first night together, thoughtfully warning me that it was time.

"Oh, my god."

Manly sperm flooded my mouth as the train shook the ground. Thomas threw back his head and fought my ankle grasp with his powerful arms pulling upwards. I pushed in opposite directions to spread his legs further apart, all the while keeping him stretched by pulling his ankles down.

Desperately, I swallowed one huge gob of his seed after another, trying my best not to choke on the endless fluid streaming down my throat. My mouth continued the back and forward stimulation on him, as though nothing new was happening. Thomas' glorious muscles twitched and rippled from my continued attack on his manhood. The mighty penis repeatedly contracted and jettisoned his cum into my eager mouth, and I was prepared to continue working on him until he asked me to stop.

Finally, the explosions began to lessen and I felt his penis becoming spongy. I released his ankles and looked up at him, but kept my mouth stationary and locked on the head of his softening unit, lightly caressing the underside with my tongue.

Thomas again smiled at me. "Let's take a break, ok?"

How thoroughly typical of us to return to mundane conversation, even after such a glorious experience. Some revelations are just too magical to discuss, because words could never completely describe them. The mutual understanding is all that is necessary.

I released him and he dropped to the ground. The caboose of the train was just now passing and Thomas laughed. "Think they saw us?"

"Who cares? If they did, it had to be a thrill for them. Bet they never saw anyone get off like that."

"God damn, Mark. That was the best thing I ever felt. Where did you learn to do that?"

"Don't know, I've never done it before. Never wanted to until now. Maybe it's just you. I kinda got into it. How about you?"

"Fuck yeah. Think we can do it again? I feel another nut coming."

"Is that a challenge?"

"No. Just want some more. No one's ever made me feel that good. I didn't know blow jobs could be anything like that. Maybe it's just you."

"It's just us, man. I think we took jacking off to a new level."

Thomas laughed. "You got that right, Markie.""You wanna get on the tree again?"

"Sounds good, but I gotta piss first."

"Me too." We stepped over to some bushes and let out a couple of long streams. I've never been excited by urine, but his dick was beautiful no matter what function it was performing. "Shake it off good, Thomas. I don't wanna taste your pee."

He stood there for a long time, carefully making sure every drop of urine had been drained. I headed back for the tree, and as I watched him respectfully clean himself for me, I felt closer to Thomas than I'd ever been to anyone before or since. Like I said before, it was just our thing. He'd do anything for me and vice versa.

Thomas walked over and jumped up to grasp his branch. He was hard in no time after I put him in my mouth. He asked me to rub his belly and chest, a task I'd wanted to perform since I met him. As we got further along, he whispered to me, "Work on my nipples."

I grabbed each one between my forefingers and thumbs. As I sucked on that perfect penis, I slowly twisted those manly nipples like they were knobs on a radio. He groaned with delight at this and I'm sure it sent testosterone throughout his body. I increased the pinching on him to see how far he wanted to go. "Back off just a little," he whispered. "Yeah, perfect." Then he closed his eyes and we were on our way.

Thomas was everything I wanted a man to be. I appreciated his silence, as I later learned how much I hated for a man to throw verbal insults my way when I serviced him. You know, like "yeah, suck that cock," or worse yet, "suck on it, bitch," that bullshit always ruined everything for me, but once you've started on a guy you gotta finish him. Sometimes I just want to say, "Shut the hell up."

So this time my buddy silently enjoyed my oral worship. I could tell when he was ready, as every wonderful muscle of his manly physique tensed up to shoot. Once more he was drained, and although he shot a manly load, it was much more manageable to take it all, a steady and even stream gently flowing into my gullet.

Now I stood up and returned Thomas' smile of satisfaction. Then he did something that nearly brought tears to my eyes. He looked at my throbbing penis, then back to me. "Do you want me to stay here for you?"

"Is it hurting you?"

"No, fool. Can't you see that I'm a he-man?"

"Keep talking like that and I'll be finished in no time."

And talk he did. He postured as though he was enduring some ungodly torture, stretching and flexing his muscles, puffing up his mighty chest and uttering manly expressions of defiance. I melted. Transferring my dick to the left hand, I approached my he-man and pretended to throw punches to his exposed gut, lightly punishing his brick wall with my knuckles. Thomas groaned and grunted at these imaginary blows, flexing his abdominals to display every line of defense. He was my manly hero in a sword and sandal epic, and I was the director of the movie.

I wanted to make it last forever, but I simply could not do it. Cum came spurting out and I shot it to the ground, making a bigger mess than I had earlier.

Thomas and I were both laughing like we were 14 again. "You wanna torture me some other way?"

"No bud, let's pack it in and save it for another day, just in case those railroad guys called in on us."

I knew he had to be drained, and I didn't want to use up all our fantasies on forced orgasms. I'd let him build up his strength and anticipate the next hook up.

So we got ourselves back together and headed for my house. He offered to let me ride his bike, but I declined so I could have a cigarette. Our conversation never approached what had just happened, just music and stupid school stuff. And of course, he had to razz me about my smoking - why did I start, why don't I quit now before it's too late, blah, blah, blah. I knew it didn't really bother him. If it had, he'd have made his request into one of our challenges. Looking back on it now, I realize this is the most important reason Thomas was my best friend. He had no pretensions and made no judgments. Wouldn't it be great if we all could approach life this way? It is a pity how adulthood soils us.

I asked my dad to take Thomas home, and they threw his bike in the back of the station wagon. I figured my buddy had to be a little exhausted, even though he would never admit it.

Six weeks and the summer passed before Thomas and I went separate ways for college. In that time I honed my cock sucking skills. We tried to be careful and not get together any more often than we had before, but any time we did, my pal Thomas got his dick professionally sucked. He'd always take off all of his clothes for me and explore new ways to be pretend tortured. After I sucked him off, he'd always pose and wait for me to finish myself. I never wanted any more from him and he could never satisfy me any other way. Those last months together were the best times of my life and could be a story unto themselves. Nothing has ever approached it before or since, and as of this day, I really don't want to share these memories with anyone else.

Thomas invited me to watch him annihilate Randy Crane. This time he used a left jab to the sternum and a right cross, which landed perfectly on the jaw. It was a work of art, watching my buddy turn his right hand just as it made impact. Timber, the smart-ass crashed to the ground and justice was served. Thomas stood over the jerk and made it clear, "Call me queer again and I'll take your fuckin' head off." Then he turned to me and smiled, that handsomely boyish grin forever emblazoned in my memory.

I wish you could have seen him strut, as we headed towards my car. He was rewarded with an all expenses paid meal from me at a nearby burger joint.

I still communicate with my pal Thomas, mostly by email, but once in a blue moon he'll call me. He got a degree in architecture and married right out of college, had a couple of kids and eventually started his own construction business. He knows I never married and he knows why, but we never talk about that. I like to think it's his fault, and I'll always love him for it.

To this day, he thanks me for helping him through high school and showing him how to jack it. I always wonder if he'll suggest hooking up, but that ball is in his court. Knowing him, he probably feels the way I do. We'll never duplicate the times we had together, and after all, there's no need to risk spoiling the priceless memories of our Sunday afternoon at Woodrow Wilson Elementary School.

Tank Books

ABOUT THE AUTHOR

Jardonn Smith is the instigator of the BDSM web site Jardonn's Erotic Tales. He writes fiction derived from his boyhood inspirations, fantasies concocted from any film or television program he saw that depicted men shirtless, bound and interrogated. As he says, "The male physique is undoubtedly handsome, but put it on a stretch rack or a cross and it becomes glorious."

This is his second collection of published short stories, his first was *I'll Never Talk: Erotic Tales of Defiant Men*. He lives in a house with a cat named Bud, much tobacco and much coffee.

www.ingramcontent.com/pod-product-compliance
Lightning Source LLC
Chambersburg PA
CBHW070757280626
47162CB00016B/1415